TRANSGALACTIC NEWSFAX (:) RANCE SPOKESMEN HAVE REVEALED THAT IN ORDER TO CONTAIN WIDE-SPREAD CIVIL DISORDER IN ROGET ESPECIALLY ANHARITTE THEY ARE DISPATCHING THIRTY DISASTER SHIPS IMMEDIATELY (:) ANHARITTE SPACEPORT HAS ALREADY BEEN ATTACKED BY RIOTERS AND A RANCE GOODWILL SHIP DESTROYED (:) THE CIVIL GOVERNMENT IS NOW REPORTED POWERLESS TO COUNTER INSURRECTION (:) FIRST TASK OF RANCE DISASTER TEAMS WILL BE TO ESTABLISH CIVIL ORDER AND REMAIN IN CONTROL UNTIL DEMOCRATIC LIBERTY IS REESTABLISHED (:) MESSAGE ENDS (:)

"Damn!" Ren looked across the blasted spaceport where even now the smoke trails persisted over the scene of devastation. The enormity of Rance's fabrication made his head spin, but his heart was seized with the cold clamp of fear.

If Alek Hardun's murder wagon had been regarded as a goodwill vessel, Ren hated to think what thirty openly operating disaster ships would bring. Despite his increasing respect for the resourceful Dion-daizan he knew that salvation this time depended on the rapid acquisition of an armed spacefleet. Presumably not even the Wizard of Anharitte could produce that.

Or could he?

THE WIZARD OF ANHARITTE

COLIN KAPP

SF
ace books
A Division of Charter Communications Inc.
A GROSSET & DUNLAP COMPANY
360 Park Avenue South
New York, New York 10010

An ACE Book

First Ace printing: February 1980

2 4 6 8 0 9 7 5 3 1
Manufactured in the United States of America

THE WIZARD OF ANHARITTE

I

Director Magno Vestevaal was glad that the space shuttle was not equipped to enter the planet Roget's atmosphere at the customary maximum velocity. The slower, powered descent gave him ample opportunity to study the terrain he was approaching. His powerful lenses and the facility offered by the shuttle's navigation dome afforded him a unique view of the sector of the planet adjacent to the spaceport. His interest had been kindled by the spacegram he had received, hinting at great trouble. Vestevaal was a firm believer in making the maximum use of information when attempting to solve a problem.

Below him now lay Anharitte, not the largest but certainly the most influential city of Roget. He could see it all with crystal clarity. To the west spread the sea, one of the great oceans dividing the planetary continents. To the north and east the landmass was largely sandy, fertile plains comprising the provinces of T'Empte, Magda, provincial Anharitte and the broad lands of T'Ampere. Beneath the city proper, the beautiful bow of the Aprillo river cut a wide channel through the sandbanks to the sea.

The city of Anharitte was based on natural geological features. The three broad hills must have been islands in a time when the oceans had

been even wider than the limits decided by their
present disposition. The hills formed a rough
triangle rising above the stubborn plains, forcing
the waters of the tributary of Daizan and several
small canals to pass between their green and granite flanks. The first hill was Anharitte itself, the
main commercial and administrative center of the
region. Even from a height the director could see
the outlines of the three great castles of Di Guaard,
Di Rode and Di Irons. Farther east along the banks
of the Aprillo rose the second hill, T'Ampere, no
longer a citadel, yet holding the major wealth of a
vast province under more than adequate control.

Situated roughly between the other hills, yet
displaced north, was the third hill. It was smaller
than its brethren and even from a height appeared
more sinister with the predominating grays and
browns of the underlying rocks. This was Magda,
key to a minor province and possessing the most
formidable fortress of all. It was with Magda, with
its paucity of approach roads and its craggy, in-
hospitable outlines, that the director was most
concerned. These lands were the realm of the man
known as the Imaiz, who, if the reports were sub-
stantiated, posed a considerable threat not only to
the composite city of Anharitte, but also to the
spaceport and the rich trade therefrom.

At the spaceport there were no formalities. All
the details such as the ship's identity and charter,
the manifest and the passenger list, had long since
been transmitted to the terminal by the shipboard
data links and the relevant cargo equipment was
already standing at the edge of the landing bowl.
As the shuttle completed touchdown procedure,
Director Vestevaal strode straight to the small

cushion-craft awaiting him. Within minutes he was clear of the limits of the spaceport.

The cushion-craft bore him along the wide sandy road of the Via Arena, the main trade road leading into Anharitte. In front of him, green and mellow in the sun, stood the broad bulk of Firsthill, bearing on its right-hand shoulder the dominating battlements of the Castle Di Guaard, frowning down on the reaches of the great Aprillo river. Slightly farther away and to the left, the darker shades of Thirdhill—the lands of Magda—rose in a dark and rather sinister contrast. It was not possible for Vestevaal to see the castle of Magda from his present location, but somewhere on those strange, broken heights was the fortress home of the Imaiz, the wizard of Anharitte, whose activities had fetched Magno Vestevaal unwillingly halfway across the universe.

Some three and a half kilometers along the Via Arena he came to the Black Rock. This marked the limit for the free use of cushion-craft. From this point on he had to—by city ordinance—engage some stavebearers whose poles would guide the craft safely through the populated streets. Because the vehicle had no positive contact with the roadway it was subject to deflection by winds and gradients. Within the city limits the stavebearers would run alongside, driving their staves occasionally into the soft undersand and forcing the fenders of the craft to run along the iron-tipped poles, thus defining and correcting the course of the floating vehicle. Progress was necessarily slow and laborious, but since power-driven wheeled vehicles were not allowed on the three hills, the visitor had no choice but to suffer it or to walk.

Just past the Arena a ragged runner, sent by the Company's agent, Tito Ren, met them and trotted ahead to guide them up the slopes of the Trade Road and through the crowded ways to the food market of Firsthill where Ren had an office. The agent paid the men off quickly, ordered house servents to collect the luggage and ushered the director into the welcome coolness of the office chambers.

While he was waiting for Vestevaal to complete his ablutions, Tito Ren watched continually out of the window that overlooked the food market, as if he were waiting for someone to appear. A half-hour later the director was refreshed and ready. He laid the spacegram purposefully on the table.

"Well, Tito, you've fetched me a long way at a most inopportune time. Whatever you have to say had better be good."

Ren turned away from his vantage point at the window.

"It will be," he said. "But the best way I can approach the intricacies of the situation is to start by showing you something. Unfortunately the time is yet a little early. Please take some wine."

"If this is a fool's errand—" Vestevaal said ominously. He did not bother to complete the sentence. He knew Ren as one of the most shrewd and efficient agents in the Company, and the long-standing association between the two men had bred a mutual trust and respect. Grumbling into his beard, Vestevaal accepted wine and came and stood by the window, looking out at the busy, colorful market.

"How long have we to wait for this great happening?" he asked.

Ren shrugged. "She would normally be here by now. But I suspect the coming of your cushion-craft will have stirred things up a bit. The one thing you can rely on in Anharitte is that every third man is a spy."

"And every third woman?" asked Vestevaal mischievously.

Ren shook his head. "The women count for almost nothing in Anharitte. Except one—and that's the one we're waiting for."

Finally becoming bored with the scene, the director turned away and began to explore the chambers. Ren remained obstinately at the window. Then a cry from the agent brought Vestevaal hastily back to follow Ren's indicating finger.

"Here's what I was waiting to show you, Director. Do you see that girl down there?"

"The tall one in the orange dress?"

"That's Zinder—a bondslave of the Castle Magda on Thirdhill. She comes to the market daily, shopping for the *Imaiz*."

"For a bondslave she's remarkably well dressed."

"For a bondslave she's remarkable in too many ways." Ren turned back into the room to face Vestevaal. "Notice how the traders treat her. Almost with deference. She may be a slave, but there's none who would dare molest her. There's not a beggar or a bondsman on the three hills who wouldn't come to her defense—even at the risk of his life."

Magno Vestevaal scowled. "Remarkable. It

shows a degree of social unity I'd not have expected in such a feudal setup."

"Great currents are at work here," said Ren. "But they run deep. A careful finger is needed to measure their pulse. It wouldn't be naive to say that Zinder somehow represents what the *Ahhn* as a race hope to become."

"A bondslave?" The director was perplexed.

"Yes, but what a bondslave! Study her carefully. Look at every detail about her—polished to perfection. Notice the dignity in the way she walks. That pose comes from confidence. And the confidence comes from thorough training and education."

"I don't see why you're making so much of her," said Vestevaal with a trace of irritation. "Many people groom their pets. I assume a slave girl in Anharitte is a legitimate part of a man's harem."

"A slavemaster's control is absolute, including control of life and death," confirmed Ren. "But I don't think you quite understood me. I said training and education."

"But you don't educate slaves—not beyond what's necessary for them to perform their duties," objected the director.

"Then one needs to speculate on just what Zinder's duties are. We haven't yet found the full measure of her abilities. She's proficient in all thirteen space languages, is apparently gifted in music and arts and has a scientific knowledge that would probably qualify her for two or three degrees at a Terran university."

"Fantastic," said Magno Vestevaal, when the implications had sunk home. He moved the curtain to gain a further look at the tall dark *Ahhn* girl who moved like a queen around the market. "How do you know so much about her, Tito?"

"I paid good Company money to the Society of Pointed Tails to have her investigated. They devised many tests of her knowledge and aptitude by way of commerce and conversation. They were more than impressed by what they found."

"How much confidence do you have in the society's report?"

"Every confidence. In Anharitte, a society must keep perfect faith with its patron. A society can refuse to accept any assignment—and frequently does to avoid conflict of interests—but once an assignment is accepted its terms and conditions become binding on its members even to the point of death. That's clan law, and its enforcement is savage."

"Accepting that for the moment, perhaps you'd explain why you felt it necessary to spend Company money investigating a slave girl?"

Ren cleared his throat. "Anharitte is a free port not only for Roget but for all ship trade spaceward into the Hub. As a space-commerce base it is priceless. The vast fortunes of the space combines and the merchant worlds have been possible very largely because of the facility offered by Anharitte as a Free Trade exchange. Make no mistake, Director, our own Company could not exist without commercial access to Anharitte."

"I'm more aware of the fact than you are," said Vestevaal, "or I would not be here now. What disturbs me is your implication that our access to Anharitte is at risk."

"I see it this way," said Ren. "Anharitte is

unique in having maintained its long-term social
stability in spite of having been exposed to space
commerce. There have been a few other free ports,
but all have succumbed to the disadvantage of
their planetary governments, requiring a dispro-
portionate share of the value of the merchandise
being shuttled through their territory. Anharitte
is different—the tolls and levies remain nominal
because they're shared only by the five aristocratic Houses: those of the Lords Di Irons, Di Rode, Di
Guaard and by the Lady T'Ampere—and by the
House of Magda. The influence of these few has
maintained a rigid social structure—albeit one
with a slave base—which has given the necessary
stability to Anharitte."

"True," said Vestevaal. "And it pays the lords
very handsomely to maintain things just as they
are. So I don't see what the problem is."

"The *Imaiz* of Magda is rocking the boat," said
Ren.

"What makes you think that?"

"Director—have you any idea what happens to
a slave-base culture when somebody starts
educating slaves to Terran graduate standard?"

"You've made your point," said Vestevaal
heavily. "Your culture becomes unstable, contaminated with ideas like democracy, civil liberty
and other corrosive notions. And finally it disin-
tegrates."

"And from the ruins somebody builds a so-
called brave new order—which is inherently
more expensive for free traders."

"Which is inherently ruinous for free traders,"
corrected Magno Vestevaal. "You were perfectly
right to call me in, Tito. This could be the biggest

threat to trade since the dissolution of the Oma-
nite empire. And you're perfectly sure that the
House of Magda is responsible?"

"There's no doubt of it. It's entirely the work of
the *Imaiz.*"

"How is the *Imaiz* different from the other lords
of Anharitte?"

"I think the clue lies in the word *Imaiz* itself.
This translates variously as wizard, wise man or
madman, depending on which *Ahhn* dialect you
speak. The suggestion is that the *Imaiz* is ac-
corded the full rights of nobility because his
magic is too potent to be ignored. The House of
Magda has a long history of congenital insanity
among its occupants—a not surprising situation
when you consider the close in-breeding that
used to take place in aristocratic houses in order
to keep the right of succession within a very narrow group.

"The persistent mental aberrations of the rulers
of Magda, usually a form of extreme mega-
lomania, have given rise to many long-standing
superstitions about the master of the fortress of
Thirdhill. One of these is that the *Imaiz* has the
ability to cast spells and control the future. History seems to show that few of Magda's occupants
were very proficient in the black arts, for all the
cruel and ingenious black rites they devised. But
the present *Imaiz* appears to be a different proposition altogether."

"You're surely not suggesting that he actually
is proficient in the black arts?"

"No. And neither is he mad. I've a different and
more dangerous picture of the current *Imaiz,*
Dion-daizan. All the evidence points to the fact

that he's cunning, ruthless, academic—and probably of Terran origin.''

"The devil!" said Vestevaal. "I thought that outworlders weren't permitted to hold land titles on Roget.''

"They aren't. There's some sort of subterfuge at work here. But the fact that he's succeeded in becoming a holder is a measure of the man we're up against.''

II

"On what sort of evidence do you base your conjecture that he's a Terran?" asked Vestevaal. "You've surely not been able to study the man himself?"

"No. We've had to content ourselves with observing Zinder. She's genuine *Ahhn* stock—but there's no academy on Roget that could give her the type of education she possesses."

"But that still leaves the possibility of the *Imaiz* being from one of the other prime worlds."

"True," admitted Ren. "But the Society of Pointed Tails is thorough in investigating such matters. During their inquiries they uncovered a most significant fact. When calculating, Zinder works in decimals to the base ten—then converts the answers to the galactic duodecimal system."

"That's nothing special," said Magno Vestevaal. "I do the same myself."

"My point entirely, Director. Your primary education was on Terra and you can't get out of the habit. Whoever trained Zinder had a similar habit. And Terra's the only planet in the universe that still clings to the base ten."

"Point taken, Tito. Your efficiency does you credit. It won't go unrewarded, I promise you. But it does look as though there's a hell of a storm brewing for Free Trade on Anharitte. From your

11

observations, does this look like part of a deliberate takeover by the House of Magda?"

"No. Far worse than that. It looks like interference with the social structure by an inveterate do-gooder more interested in the welfare of the bottom four-fifths of the population than he is in legitimate profit."

" 'Curse all saviours of the human race—for they are responsible for most of the blacker parts of history!' " quoted Vestevaal despondently. He moved back to the window and began to watch the tall slave girl again, now examining her every movement with a wiser interest. "Damn it, Tito, you know we can't let this happen, don't you?"

"I know it," said Ren. "That's the reason I called you in. I want permission, financing and backing to organize an opposition to the *Imaiz*."

"Interference with the internal politics of an independent planet is an extremely dangerous business."

"But it wouldn't be the first time it has been done. Nor is what I propose strictly interference. It could rather be viewed as assistance in maintaining the existing balance of power. The Lords Di Rode and Di Guaard and the Lady T'Ampere are scarcely going to side with the *Imaiz* and risk their income if not their lives if a revolution comes. Di Irons is the city prefect. He's a bit of an unknown quantity in this, but he's responsible for law and order, so I doubt if he'll reject our assistance in maintaining the *status quo*. Most of the societies grow fat under the present regime, so they're not going to welcome change either. And I'm sure the planetary government would love to have us thwart a provincial uprising for them—if it were done with discretion. That puts the major percentage of wealth, influence and interests on our side. Give me the facilities and I'll crush the *Imaiz* without leaving even a ripple on the surface."

"Not so fast, Tito. We're not the only Company affected—or even the largest. And we've the merchant worlds to consider. Before we take any action that might affect the future of Anharitte as a free port we're going to need the approval of the Free Trade Council—most particularly as insurance in case the venture goes sour on us. And before I dare approach the council I have to be absolutely certain that what you've told me is the truth. Not that I'm doubting you, of course, but it would be embarrassing if we were being manipulated into doing the dirty work for somebody who had a simple grudge against the *Imaiz*."

"I appreciate your caution. If you wish I'll arrange for the senior scribes of the Society of Pointed Tails to meet you so that you can question them directly."

"No need for that," said Magno Vestevaal. "I think I can satisfy myself more easily." He moved toward the door.

"What had you in mind?" Ren rose to follow him.

"I'm going downstairs, of course. To have a word with Zinder."

Ren's eyebrows rose. "I wouldn't advise it. And for God's sake—remember she's well protected."

"It was the truth of that proposition I wished to test. If that fact holds true, then the rest of the story holds true."

Tito Ren sighed and reached for his sword belt.

He paused only to fasten the ornate buckle before he followed the director out into the street.

The emergence of the two outworlders into the brilliant sunshine at the edge of the square—the director purposefully striding towards Zinder, and Ren following—caused an immediate thrill of interest to run through the market place. There was a quieting in the pace of the bargaining, though each man pretended still to be about his business. The agent sensed rather than saw the evasive group of figures who moved to strategic positions in the crowd, prepared for trouble. Worst of all was the unspoken wariness of the merchants, traditionally neutral in political affairs. If Vestevaal forced the incident into an affray, then even the dour men of small commerce seemed likely to side with Zinder.

Ren normally had complete confidence in Vestevaal's ability to contain a crisis. However, Ren was from habit more attuned to the local undercurrents in Anharitte than Vestevaal could be. Purely from lack of "feel" of the situation the director might provoke an explosive incident. Under his tunic Ren could feel the comforting weight of his blaster. He would hesitate to use the weapon in such a populated place, but, if necessity demanded, he could drop a dozen men with a single charge.

"You there! Girl—come here." Vestevaal was approaching Zinder, calling imperiously. She turned her head and waited for him, her face composed, as if the meeting were an event not unexpected.

The director stopped suddenly as he realized

she intended that he must be the one to walk the intervening distance if he wished to speak with her. She plainly did not propose to come to him.

"I said come," said Vestevaal, knowing the delicate dictates of slave etiquette.

She looked him up and down with shrewd appraisal, then turned back to the merchant at whose stall she was and continued her transaction. The director sensed that all eyes were upon him and wondered how he would resolve the offered slight. It was unthinkable for any slave other than Zinder to have disobeyed a public command from a man so obviously a prominent outworlder. Vestevaal realized that he had trapped himself into an open contest of wills. He could not afford to let the matter pass.

He strode angrily across the remaining distance and caught hold of her left wrist, on which the slave mark was indelibly written. At close quarters she was attractive rather than beautiful in the classic sense. Her dark hair framed a strong face, which displayed an unassailable character. But more impressive was the rich by-play of emotions continuously monitored in her eyes.

"I thought so—the House of Magda." Vestevaal was emphasizing the aspect of bondage, trying to draw a reaction. "Your master will be hearing from me. You're the one they call Zinder, aren't you?"

"But of course, Director Vestevaal. But then you knew that before you came across here. Indeed, I am the reason you came." Her voice was clear and melodious, modulated with a subtle artistry. Her speech was perfectly articulated Terran in which the attractive lilt of the native *Ahhn* accent had been carefully preserved. "But I'm glad you did come. Peering from behind a curtain is rather undignified for a man of your standing with the Free Trade Council."

"Damn!" said Vestevaal, knowing that he was now the center of an attentive audience. "You take much on yourself, girl. Not only do you open wounds, but you also apply salt."

"Salt? Only to the wounds of enemies," she answered easily. "Among friends salt is for sharing at table. If I've offered salt, Director, it's you who have chosen how to use it."

In her deep eyes was no fear or displeasure, only an engaging challenge. Behind the eyes were limitless funds of resourcefulness. Though her lips were smiling slightly, they showed neither insolence nor arrogance. She was meeting him on an equal level and both of them knew it. What had started as a deliberate confrontation had ended in a rout for Vestevaal. His wry smile of admiration turned into a great gust of laughter and he reached this time for her right hand and kissed it.

"As you so rightly said, Zinder, it was I who chose how to use the salt. But whereas a man can mostly choose his friends, circumstances choose his enemies for him. There are times when one could wish the reverse. Please present my compliments to the Imaiz—and tell him that if ever he wishes to dispose of your bond he will find in myself an eager purchaser."

"I will convey your words to Dion-daizan. I'm sure he'll be both amused and flattered."

"And also tell him that I mean to stop him by every means at my disposal."

"That isn't news, Director Vestevaal. Had he not been convinced of it he would not have bothered sending me here today."

"He anticipated this meeting?"

"The chance of this or something like it was highly probable. He felt it only fair you should know the character of the opposition."

"He could scarcely have made the point more strongly."

"What else would you expect of the wizard of Anharitte?"

She bowed respectfully and moved away like a colorful flower among the stalls, the barest hint of triumph on her lips. The tension that had held the cluttered market in a long hiatus drained slowly away and the noisy chatter of bargaining returned. Ren, who had been silent to this moment, moved to the director's elbow.

"I told you I didn't advise it," he said critically.

"You were right, Tito," Magno Vestevaal told him. "I should have listened to you more carefully. Mark that round to the credit of the *Imaiz*. If that's a sample of his tactics we'll be needing more than moral support from the Free Trade Council."

"Then you're satisfied with my assessment of the situation?"

"Send word to have the shuttle readied for blast-off as soon as I reach it. I'll be calling an emergency session of the council and asking for their backing with all the facilities we need. With the evidence I shall give them I doubt there will even be a debate. In the meantime, you're in charge here. You have my authority to draw whatever Company funds you need. Stop the

Imaiz, neutralize his policy or just plain kill him—I don't mind which. But if he turns many more slaves like Zinder loose in Anharitte, we're surely going to have another democracy on our hands. And what will become of Free Trade then?''

III

To understand the function of the societies in Anharitte it was necessary to view them against the background of the uneasy truce local feudalism maintained. The burgeoning space technology barely thrust outside the city's limits. Almost alone among the institutions of Anharitte, the societies had been forced to adapt to the twin pressures and now formed a precarious link at once joining and keeping separate the rival ways of life.

Historically the societies has been clans of skilled mercenary soldiers who offered their services to any who found it beneficial to use hired arms rather than maintain their own forces. In either attacking or defensive roles, the clans had played a great part in the early formation of the "kingdoms" from which the great Houses of Roget had emerged after the adoption of central government.

With the coming of less turbulent times the societies had found new exercise for their warlike crafts. When the thriving communities had outgrown the protection afforded by the great castles on the three hills, the merchants outside the citadels had become exposed to attacks by Tyrene pirates who came up the broad Aprillo river. Many merchants had then found it expedient to use the armed services of the societies to protect their homes and warehouses. From this had evolved the contract system whereby a merchant engaged a society for protection but paid for the service only as and when it was required. This function, too, sharpened the efficiency of the societies themselves, because the best protection contracts went to the clans with the proven ability to preserve the life and wealth of their patrons.

As piracy became a less profitable profession, the idea of contract protection remained. Always adaptable, the societies were swift to monitor the change and quick to evolve new services to offer. Slave control in the expanding estates was an obvious extension. The passing of two disastrous plagues brought about the introduction of society hospitals. Frequent fires in the huddled wooden buildings caused the initiation of society fire services. Thus the outworld concept of insurance found a more personal and practical analogue in Anharitte.

Yet the warrior function of the societies was not forgotten. A man with the price might still arrange for the skilled disposal of his rival or the waging of a feud with an enemy. While the taking of life in Anharitte was not necessarily a crime, disturbance of the peace of the city was an offense. The societies learned to conduct their affairs with great discretion under the grim and scowling eyes of a prefecture which neither approved nor disapproved of what they did—provided the quiet life of the city was maintained.

The coming of the spaceport had further enhanced the societies' role. No outworlders were permitted to hold property titles on Roget—a necessary precaution for a culture intending to preserve its own identity in the face of commercial outworld interests—but there was nothing to stop outworlders entering into contracts with a society and leasing buildings held in the society's name. The same applied to slave-bonds and to every other form of transaction that had to be registered with the prefecture. Thus the societies, inextricably part of the old culture, became also the bridgehead of the new.

As a Company agent more astute than most, Tito Ren had long since learned the value of an in-depth study both of the history and the cultural mores of the territories to which he was assigned. Thus he had been quick to recognize the multiple role of the societies and equally quick to adapt the system to his own requirements. His researches had shown the Society of Pointed Tails to be not only the most efficient of the available clans, but also the one still most proficient in the use of arms in situations where the rudimentary laws of Roget could not be bent sufficiently to gain the necessary advantage for an ambitious free trader.

Ren had wooed the members of Pointed Tails by concentrating his considerable leasings of property, services and local labor with them. He pursued his advantage by offering them well-paid investigation assignments probing those aspects of life in Anharitte he found of interest. Now he was ready to move into the next phase—that of actually using the Pointed Tails as an instrument with which to manipulate particular elements of Anharitte society itself. He was prepared to recognize, however, that a society as competent as the Pointed Tails would not be likely to accept his propositions without question. Nor was he wrong.

Catuul Gras, senior scribe of the Society of Pointed Tails, looked questioningly at Ren.

"You've already spoken with your director, then?"

"I have—and he's in complete agreement. The *Imaiz* will have to be stopped. The director has already given me access to whatever Company funds I need in order to make a preliminary approach to you—and now he has gone to consult with the Free Trade Council. If they concur, I'll have unlimited funding from the Galactic Bank itself and whatever additional facilities I choose to call on."

"And you wish the Pointed Tails to prepare a scheme of harassment and feud against Diondaizan?"

"I need more than a feud. I need to crush Diondaizan. Harassment may have its place—but if it doesn't bring results I'm prepared to consider anything short of full-scale warfare."

"And the Prefect Di Irons? Do you think he's going to sit by happily while you wage war on the *Imaiz*?"

"I intend to seek the support of all the lords of Anharitte, Di Irons among them. If we can gain their backing plus that of the Free Trade Council, the *Imaiz* won't stand a chance."

Catuul, his brilliant robes flowing about his muscled body, took a pensive turn around Ren's booklined chamber. He was obviously not enthusiastic.

"I think you oversimplify about the lords," he

said. "Di Irons will never support you in an overt act of war against the *Imaiz*, whatever his private sympathies. Di Guaard is so insane he's still holding an inquisition to find pirates who became extinct two generations ago. Di Rode will listen to you, but he's unlikely actively to support an outworlder against another House of Anharitte. Only the Lady T'Ampere appears as a possible ally—though I doubt you'd be prepared to pay her price for the alliance."

"And the Society of Pointed Tails?" asked Ren. "Will they support me?"

Catuul frowned. "I can't anticipate the decision of my fellow scribes. I'll call an immediate meeting of the lodge and recommend they take your assignment. But there will be much argument."

"What's there to argue about?"

"About the possibility of losing the fight. It's easy enough for you to wave money and say you want to crush the *Imaiz*. But did you never think that Dion-daizan may prove powerful enough to crush the lot of us?"

"That isn't possible," said Ren. "Because whatever strengths he has, I can call on resources to match his ten times over. This is one fight you can't possibly lose."

"Your thinking is typical of an outworlder's," said Catuul. "You don't appreciate Dion's considerable influence with the bondslaves—or his command of magic. Believe me, you underestimate his potential, or you would not so lightly engage in plans for his destruction."

"Dion-daizan is a fraud. He's a Terran adventurer—with no more occult powers than you or I."

Catuul shrugged. "Call him by any name you
like. We know him as a formidable and unforgiv-
ing enemy. He never allows an injury to pass
unavenged."

"I can always approach another society if the
Pointed Tails have cowards among their members," said Ren coldly.

"Cowards?" Catuul swung on him angrily.
"There are none braver or more dedicated than
the Pointed Tails. It isn't they who might falter—
but you."

"I?" Ren was perplexed.

"Of course. If the society accepts your assignment every man is committed to the death. But
you have the option to rescind the contract at any
time. If the going gets too rough you can retreat
offworld to lick your wounds and total up your
losses. But we can't. We have to continue operating here in Anharitte—and the *Imaiz* makes no
distinction between those who are paid to injure
him and those who do the paying. Only the scrolls
tell of the remains of societies who once tangled
with the *Imaiz* and lost."

"Nevertheless," said Ren, "that isn't going to
happen. If ever I drew back, the Free Trade Council would replace me with another. They can't
afford to do otherwise. And their resources have
no limit—they can acquire them a thousand times
faster than we can exhaust them. I'm offering you
the backing of a dozen merchant worlds and
seven hundred space companies and combines—
to fight one man and a handful of slaves. Tell that
to the other scribes and see if they share your
doubts."

"I'll tell them," said Catuul gravely, gathering

his robe across his arm. "And I think they'll be convinced. But it will be a close decision. I'll let you have our answer in the morning."

When Catuul had departed Ren turned his attention to the radio link with the space terminal. From the spaceport the powerful FTL communications equipment reached out in real time to the relay chains across the vastness of commercial interstellar space. In response to his inquiry he learned that an incoming call from Free Trade Central was already logged a mere five hours away. Finally Vestevaal's voice came through.

"Tito, can you hear me clearly?"

"Yes, Director. Transmission is good. Did the council meeting go in your favor?"

"It did indeed. They were even more perturbed than we—especially those who have big investments nearer the Rim. The outcome is that we've got all the support we need. The Galactic Bank will give you unrestricted credit. Any Free Trade ships calling at Anharitte will be obliged to offer assistance—and the merchant worlds of Combien and Rance are donating a light battle cruiser to be set down on Anharitte for the duration of the exercise. The battle cruiser will have most of the facilities you might require in the way of laboratories, trained commandos, communications, armaments and the like. You've enough there to start a war if you should need to."

"It mustn't come to that," said Ren. "If we upset the planetary government we'll be thrown off Roget for sure. Our best chance is to try to woo the local lords to our side, then to fight an undercover campaign against the Imaiz. Then we can divide

Magda's share of the spaceport royalties among
the remaining Houses and expect the dust to settle
pretty fast."

"You're the man on the spot, Tito, so it's your
advice that counts. I'll be returning to Roget
shortly, but purely as an observer and to maintain
liaison with the Free Trade Council. I may advise
on policy, but the strategy and conduct of the
battle will be entirely your affair. I hope that arrangement is to your liking."

"I couldn't have asked for better. Terran or no
Terran, if we have modern weapons and the support of the other lords, the *Imaiz* hasn't got a
chance."

"I wish I completely shared your confidence,"
said Magno Vestevaal, signing off. "But Zinder
didn't have to make that confrontation in the market. For the moment I almost wondered if the
Imaiz wasn't spoiling for a fight."

Catuul Gras came back the next morning with
the Pointed Tails' acceptance of the offer. The
price was high, but Ren brushed aside the financial considerations. "You managed to find
agreement, then?"

Catuul grimaced. "Some of the scribes had reservations, but they're all alarmed by what the
Imaiz is doing. Certainly they respond to your
argument that if we're to maintain things in
Anharitte as they now stand, some form of action
is necessary to curtail Dion-daizan. The fact that
you're willing to finance and supply backing for
the skirmish makes it easier for us to do what we
should finally have been forced to do anyway. In
some ways this is an alliance—and there are other
societies who may contribute to our cause."

Ren held out his hand in acceptance of the bargain. "Then it's settled. The *Imaiz* will be stopped."

"He will be. But initially we must proceed by customary feud and harassment. Only if these measures aren't effective can we consider outright war."

"I'll accept that," said Ren. "You start to prepare a campaign against the *Imaiz*. I'll do some preliminary canvassing for support among the other lords. I suggest we meet again in two days' time to decide our plan of action."

As Ren left his office he was at once aware of being observed. He had not gone far through the quaint and narrow streets before a prefecture watchman approached him.

"Agent Ren?"

"The same." The watchman had obviously been waiting for him to emerge. "What services can I offer?"

"If you please, you will accompany me to the prefecture. Lord Di Irons wishes to speak with you."

"And I with him," said Ren, though he recognized the summons for the imperious demand that it was. If he had thought of declining the invitation the appearance of two more watchmen behind him pointed up the wisdom of cheerful compliance.

Even in the bright sun the prefecture looked cold and uninviting. The wide portals shaded the exterior brilliance quickly into a dim chill that seemed resident in the very fabric of the building. Tito Ren could not repress a shiver as he entered the main door. The stone corridors of the law were always anathema to him.

Di Irons' office was large and grimly impressive. On the same scale was the man himself. Huge, bearded, and with a shock of rust-red, unruly hair, he was as unlike the typical *Ahhn* as was Ren himself. His very presence spoke of strength and granite resolution. The prefect was obviously not a man to be lightly deflected from his task.

"Agent Ren—" the handshake was a mere formality—"I've asked you here because we need a better understanding of each other. My job is to maintain the law in Anharitte. Yours is to run a profitable exchange of trade through our sea and spaceport facilities. It would be a pity if in pursuit of our respective duties we should happen to collide."

"Indeed a pity." Ren shifted uncomfortably on his chair. "However, I think the possibility is slight. We traders are aware that we remain here on sufferance."

"Don't fence with me," said Di Irons savagely. "I spoke of understanding. We both know that the lords of Anharitte are as much dependent on your money as you are upon access to the free port facilities. So let's speak frankly. I know that you and your director intend making feud with the *Imaiz*."

Ren examined his inquisitor warily. "You know of that?"

"Of course. Not much occurs in Anharitte that isn't known in the prefecture. Whether or not we choose to act on what we know depends on our interpretation of the law. Provocation isn't an offense. But if Vestevaal had struck Zinder the other day we'd have been very much concerned."

"To protect a slave?" Ren affected a measure of surprise he did not feel.

Di Irons' voice was quieter now but just as dangerous. "No. We would have had to intervene to protect your stupid hides. And that offends our idea of preservation of the peace. You're no stranger here, Ren. You know which way the tides flow in Anharitte."

"I know it," said Ren, "but the director needed proof of my interpretation."

"Well, I gather he got it. But I don't advise him to make an open confrontation like that again. Zinder has too many sympathizers to make it a healthy pastime. But what escapes me is why your director needed proof of her ability to cut him down to size."

"Because it's my contention that if the *Imaiz* continues to educate slaves to her level, the slave structure will crumble. Your society as it now exists will crumble. Don't ask me what will replace it—but it will certainly be a system with less tolerance toward Free Trade than the one we enjoy at the moment."

"So that's it." Di Irons was suddenly caught by the speculation.

"You asked for understanding," said Ren. "Well, I've shown my blade. Now dare you return the gesture? I don't imagine you lords of Anharitte would look upon the withdrawal of Free Trade with much favor."

"No!" Di Irons reacted violently. "You'll not involve me in politics. The *Imaiz* may be ill advised in the way he treats his slaves. But if I were to take arms against every slavemaster I considered ill advised, I would not have half enough cells in which to hold them—or a tenth enough tormentors to make their stay uncomfortable. In any case, I think you're reading more into this than is written. I know Dion well. He's a frequent guest in my household."

"And Zinder? Is she a frequent guest, too? A slave?"

"If Dion wills it. A slavemaster's rights over his bondslaves are absolute—and that's a principle I must uphold. If he chooses to pretty her and pamper her it's no concern of mine. She would not be the first bondslave to become a favored concubine—though I'll not say that's what she is. If Dion is pleased to bring her to my table I'll be the last to interfere. In any case, Zinder's a charming and cultured girl."

"And you approve of a bondslave's being educated to this level?"

"I don't necessarily approve when a master has a slave stoned to death for some imagined slight. My function is not to judge but to maintain the law. Thus far I've no evidence that Dion-daizan has broken it."

"Then you're not willing to assist us in protecting Anharitte from the *Imaiz's* slave policy?"

"I'm not even convinced there is any threat. A man who owns slaves must always be on guard against rebellion—and I fancy Dion runs less risk of this than most. But above all, the law must be neutral—or it ceases to be law and becomes tyranny. Let it not be said that a prefect of Anharitte used his position to persecute others on the word of an outworld merchant's agent.

"If you think you have a grievance against Dion-daizan you can have recourse to the supreme court in Gaillen. Or you can attempt to achieve satisfaction through the services of a society. But let them advise you on tactics. The societies know how to operate with discretion. If your feud moves into the public realm I shall act—and act decisively and without favor. Do I make myself clear?"

"Would you also move against the *Imaiz* if the necessity arose?"

"The lords of Anharitte have certain rights of arms. Outside those, whoever destroys the peace of Anharitte will be forced to account to me. That goes for the *Imaiz*, for the other lords—and most especially for you, Ren. Agent you may be, but if you assume the role of *agent provocateur*, then you'll not find us so hospitable."

Ren scowled with disappointment. "I doubt the other lords would condone your tolerance toward the activities of Dion-daizan and his slaves."

The prefect exploded in anger. "You're an outworlder, Ren. Don't try and tell me what Di Rode and Di Guaard and the Lady T'Ampere would or wouldn't think. I was raised with these people. I know what they think better than they know it themselves."

"But you weren't raised with the *Imaiz*," said Ren coldly. "Because the suggestion is very strong that he's a Terran. Don't tell me that doesn't offend your precious law?"

For the first time Di Irons seemed unsure of himself.

"You have evidence to support that statement?"

"No positive proof as yet. But I will have. Don't you query the rights of the claimants to your aristocratic Houses?"

"Query?" Di Irons was grimly amused. "Do you

think I would dare look closely at the credentials of Di Rode or Di Guaard—or they at mine? How many murdered infants do you suppose would be found in the moats? Which unfortunate son went alive into his tomb behind the new wall in the tower? Whose mother is that demented crone who has sat in chains for thirty years in the dungeon? The rights of the title go to the claimant with the ability to survive at the top. The state acknowledges the title of the House—the holder of the title declares himself."

"I understand all that," said Ren patiently. "But surely the position is different if the occupant of the title is an outworlder?"

"It would be—if the matter could be proved. Then I would have to act. But you've admitted you don't have the evidence. Until you do, I submit you're playing a very dangerous game."

"Dangerous in what way?" asked Ren.

"I know Dion well. He's shrewd, resourceful—and his information is impeccable. What do you think he'll be doing while you wander the countryside trying to stir trouble against him? I strongly advise you to guard your back, not to visit dark places alone and to engage a taster to test your food. If you were to die—I'm sure I'd have a hard time trying to hang the responsibility on Dion-daizan."

"I'll remember that. But in the meantime, think over what I've said. I doubt even you would refuse a quarter of Magda's share of the income from the spaceports concession."

"I prize some things above money," said Di Irons. "And one of them is life. Nobody in his senses provokes a needless quarrel with a man as far-reaching and formidable as Dion-daizan. I know it's not fashionable among Free Traders to speak of magic and superstitions, but some of the works of the *Imaiz* are well beyond the powers of man."

"That I must yet have proved to me," said Tito Ren. "For the moment I prefer to regard him merely as an academic Terran adventurer with no supernatural powers."

"It would be churlish of me," said Di Irons, "not to wish you a successful venture. If what you've told me is true I stand to gain or lose as much as you. But I would need more reason than you've given before I raised my hand against the wizard of Anharitte. Take care, merchant. You've chosen a stronger enemy than you think."

The conversation was interrupted by a knock on the door. A watchman came in, apologized for the intrusion and handed Di Irons a note. The latter read it, looked questioningly at Ren for a moment—then his face broke into a wry smile.

"It appears I spoke more truly than I knew. Don't tell me after this that you don't believe in the powers of the *Imaiz*."

"Why? What happened?"

"You rent a bonded oil and spirit warehouse on the quayside of Firstwater?"

"I do." Ren was half on his feet. "What's the trouble?"

"It's on fire," said Di Irons. "You had best get down there. I think this will not be the last conversation we'll be having on the matter, so you have my permission to proceed. But tomorrow I'll be asking questions. I don't tolerate the destruction of property in a private feud—and if I find proof that either you or Dion-daizan has done this deliberately, an accounting will have to be made."

"I'm not likely to set fire to my own warehouse," said Ren bitterly.

"And Dion's not stupid enough to indulge in ordinary arson," said Di Irons. "Or in any event, I've never been able to prove he is. If you find me some proof, Ren, I'll guarantee to lay it where it belongs."

IV

Ren thought of returning to his chambers for his cushion-craft. Then he realized that the poling of the vehicle by stavebearers through the city streets and down the Trade Road would be a slow and tiresome business. A mule cart would be quicker—but not much. The total distance from the prefecture to Firstwater was no greater than two kilometers and much of the way lay down the slopes of Firsthill into the valley formed with Thirdhill on the other shore. Overall he calculated he could make the journey more quickly on foot and he set out at a labored jog—with complete disregard for lack of dignity or sweat.

He had barely cleared the fringes of the buildings and come out at the end of the Trade Road overlooking Firstwater when he became aware of the broad smoke column rising into the sultry air. If he had thought the fire might only be a minor one his surmise was soon corrected. Even through the dense smoke cloud he could see the bright seat of the flame—and its visibility at this distance told him that the conflagration must be total as far as his installation was concerned.

The Trade Road was easy to negotiate. Such carts as were on it were also moving downhill, laden with spectators eager to witness the fire. Most of these vehicles, braked with iron wedges

and chains against the slope, were easily over-
taken, and his urgent running riased a great deal
of amused comment. On the Via Arena the crowds
thickened and the road to Magda Crossing was
nearly impassable in the direction of the river.
Fortunately a group of Pointed Tails met him and
forged him a path through the mobs to a point
near the burning warehouse.

The Pointed Tails' fire appliance was there—
with all its hand-cranked absurdity. It was so obviously inadequate against the roaring inferno
that it had not been put into even token use. Two
other societies had also brought their appliances,
but these were equally useless and stood well
clear of the outer perimeter fence, where they
would not be affected by the intense heat.

The fire itself was overwhelming. The whole
building, with walls of massive stone blocks, vi-
brated with the tremendous roar of the furnace
within. The structure had no windows, and the
two exterior doors jetted streams of angry flame
like enormous blowlamps. The roof, once a structure of heavily tarred wood, was completely gone.
Surmounting the walls was a continuous crown
of fire, which produced such intense heat that the
spectators had to move back repeatedly to avoid
being scorched.

The warehouse had two perimeter fences, one
contained within the other, but it was now impossible to approach the building nearer than the
confines of the outer fence. Here Ren found Catuul
Gras, his face heavy red from the heat. Catuul was
watching the progress of the conflagration with
frank disbelief. His expressive glance at Ren
suggested both physical and mental agony. He
gestured toward his own useless fire appliance.

"I took the liberty of calling on the spaceport for emergency assistance. I hope I did right."

"Exactly right," approved Ren. "How did the fire start?"

"We don't know. No goods have moved in or out of the warehouse for fifteen days. Everything was secure on the last round of the society guards and the picket between the fences has been strictly maintained. The fire started behind locked doors and we're certain that nobody could have entered."

"Could some sort of time fuse or incendiary mechanism have been placed inside?"

Catuul grimaced. "I know of no device obtainable hereabouts with such a long delay. But if you're thinking this is the work of the Imaiz you pose a paradox. Those doors were sealed several days before your quarrel with Dion-daizan became actual. You could only suspect his hand if you were prepared to credit him with the magical powers you deny he possesses."

"Nevertheless, the timing's too perfect to be a matter of coincidence. Even Di Irons hinted he suspected that the Imaiz was behind it. Well, if it is Dion's work and there's any evidence left to prove it, it will give us a good start for our harassment. Di Irons is all set to string up the Imaiz by the thumbs if he's found responsible for the destruction of property during a private feud. All he needs is proof—and here come the boys who can give it to us."

Movement among the watchers on the road signaled the arrival of the cushioncraft emergency tender from the spaceport. Behind it came two more tenders containing compound foam and chemicals. They were deftly manipulated into place. In complete contrast to the laughable native fire appliances, these three vehicles, normally reserved for spacecrash emergencies, were magnificently equipped and manned by trained and competent crews. Within seconds the great pumps were working and hoses were being run out as far as the river to bring in the additional water necessary to complete the work of the foam coverage.

Pictor Don, the spaceport's emergency commander, spared neither Ren nor Catuul a glance as he deployed his facilities for maximum effect. The foam from the hoses hit the side of the building and wherever it touched it solidified into glass slag and instantly formed an air-excluding seal that was also an impressive heat-reducing barrier. The properties of the solidifying foam were such that it could easily withstand the temperatures involved, while its noncommunicating cellular structure was light, yet strong enough to prevent the collapse of all but the heaviest parts of buildings. In dealing with a fire of these proportions the shell of the building could literally be filled with foam in a matter of minutes with a hundred percent expectation of complete extinction of the fire.

The radiated heat fell away dramatically as the foam blanket coated the walls and the forecourt. Ren and Catuul followed the fire team nearer as the work of filling the building's shell with foam began. After a short while, however, they became aware that something was wrong—the flames in the interior, instead of yielding, had become concentrated in one central spot and now roared like a volcano. The flare hurled large pieces of congealed foam high into the air to fall at a distance, to the intense consternation of the onlookers.

Finally Pictor Don dropped down from his command point and came over to Ren.

"What have you got in there, Tito? Rocket fuel?"

The agent shook his head. "No. Mainly high-grade crude oils and essential oils waiting shipment offworld to Rance for refining."

"But the oxidants," protested Don. "You should know better than to store oxidants with flammables."

"There are no oxidants there. In fact, no tonnages of oxidants are available on Roget."

Pictor Don shook his head. "That foam can extinguish anything up to and including a blazing well-head without trouble. But you've got something in there that could have put the whole building comfortably into orbit had the jet been pointed down instead of up. A few tons of liquid oxygen would do the trick with your high-grade oil—but without oxygen you couldn't produce a flare like that in a million years."

"No oxygen," said Ren. "There's not a liquid oxygen plant within sixteen light-years of Roget and it's a dead certainty that oxygen is not imported."

A cry from a member of the fire team indicated that the situation was changing. Pictor Don returned to his post and Ren saw the bright plume of flame above the building gradually diminish and finally become extinguished by the solidifying foam. The fire was out.

"What happens now?" asked Catuul.

"First they extract the heat from the surface by cooling the mass with water. Then they progressively add alkali to the water and this slowly dissolves the foam. By control of what they spray they can stop the process at any point to allow the removal of potentially dangerous masonry or to inspect for signs of arson before the evidence is too much disturbed."

The fire team was now spraying river water from its hoses, but such was the heat-insulating effectivness of the cellular mass that very little of the intense heat still trapped below the surface was available to be carried away by the water. Pictor Don mounted a hydraulic hoist and climbed from it to the surface of the foam filling the building's walls. The strength of the glasslike substance was such that his weight barely dented the surface. He scrunched over almost the entire area of the warehouse on a quick tour of inspection.

He ordered alkali to be applied. About a thirty-centimeter layer of the foam was stripped from the surface by chemical leaching. Newly exposed fragments of the building were cooled with water and a second round of inspection followed.

Then the emergency commander approached the edge of the building and called over the wall. "Get Tito Ren up here—and that Pointed Tail fellow."

Somewhat reluctantly Ren and Catuul Gras allowed themselves to be conducted to the hoist and raised to the top of the wall. There was something unnerving about stepping onto a layer of foam that had been a sprayable liquid such a short

time before. The surface felt alarmingly fragile.
Overcoming their fears, however, the two walked
across the crunching surface toward Pictor Don.
At a certain point he cautioned them to stop.

"Mind where you put your feet in that area just
in front of you. There's a giant bubble in the foam
reaching, as far as I can judge, right down to base
level. That was the blowhole through which the
last flame persisted. Unless I miss my guess, the
root cause of the fire lies directly at the bottom end
of that bubble. Does its position give you any
clues?"

Catuul glanced around at the fragments of
outer wall visible above the foam, trying to verify
his bearings. "We're located over what was the
inner storeroom."

"What was kept up there?"

"The high-grade crude oil," said Ren.

"In metal tanks?"

"No. Wooden barrels. It's the only way the native producers will package it. Wharfage facilities
don't run to the accommodation of tankers."

"Wasn't there anything else?" Pictor Don was
completely unconvinced.

"Nothing," said Ren. "I counted the barrels myself. We were going to repackage the whole con-
signment in spaceweight containers ready for
shipment. And every single barrel was broached
to obtain analysis samples, so I can guarantee that
the store contained nothing but high-grade oil."

"Very well." Pictor Don's voice still carried no
evidence of conviction. He indicated that they
should all return to the ground. The chemical
stripping of the foam began again, with interrup-
tions at intervals for repeated inspections. Finally

Don again called for Ren and Catuul Gras.

The thickness of the foam had been reduced to a meter. The space around the blowhole had been completely cleared for a radius of several meters. Ren and his colleague were now able to inspect the area Pictor Don regarded as the base of the fire.

"A drain—" Ren regarded the charred and blackened area of the floor with astonishment.

"Yes." Don was critical. "A drain you used to take the overspill of oil during the sampling of the barrels for analysis, perhaps?"

"There was some oil spillage," agreed Ren. "But I don't see—"

"Where does the drain lead?"

"To the river, I should hope."

Seconds later he was running across the broad forecourt toward the river, a sudden suspicion in his mind. The banks were complex with piers and moorings and wharves, but hard against the bank protruded one particular pipe whose end even now drained black dregs from the disastrous fire. The marks of a coupling that had been placed over the pipe's end were plainly visible—the coupling itself was gone, along with the craft that undoubtedly had born it.

Angrily Ren scanned the river. The slow drift of barges and ships—left toward the spaceport and right toward the shipping lanes and the sea—was a complex movement that defied analysis. The number of barges and ships provided too much information for Ren to be able to determine which craft might be equipped with couplings to hold against his particular drain and discharge tonnage quantities of oxidant under pressure into the interior of the warehouse. Here was plain evidence of sabotage, but no proof of the sort that could be used to point a finger at Dion-daizan.

"It was a honey of a scheme," Ren said later in grudging admiration. "We'll never convince Di Irons of the truth—"

Pictor Don had himself lowered on a cradle down to the entrance of the pipe. Here he explored with an instrument.

"The water from the hosedown has washed out all real evidence," he said. "But I'd guess somebody's been feeding pure oxygen up this pipe—and I'd say the probability was high that it was obtained by boiling off liquid oxygen."

"And the ignition?" asked Ren.

"They wouldn't need to bother. The oil would ignite spontaneously as the oxygen concentration went up. You've been rather cleverly sabotaged, Tito."

"And no prizes for guessing by whom," said Ren morosely.

"I thought you said there was no tonnage oxygen available on Roget?"

"There are no plants that we're aware of, Pictor. Native industry isn't that far advanced. But I'm wondering if there aren't oxygen facilities in Castle Magda. A good Terran technician supplied with the sort of money the spaceport dues provide shouldn't have too much trouble building a liquid oxygen plant—or any other technical facility, when you come to think of it."

"But I don't see," said Catuul Gras, "how it could be known that putting something up that particular pipe would result in a fire in our warehouse. There are hundreds of similar pipes to choose from. In any case, the drain at the other end of the pipe might not have been in the right position."

"I think I know how that was decided," said Ren. "Somebody worked out the details of that episode from inside the warehouse." He indicated the gang of slaves now filing back into the warehouse compound ready to start the work of demolition and clearance.

"If the Imaiz could bring Zinder to Terran graduate standard, how many other slaves has he similarly educated and then resold? It's slightly unnerving to think that we could have one or two graduate chemists working as bondslaves in our establishments. Think what an effective fifth column that would make. Is it possible, Catuul, that we've acquired some slaves the Imaiz might have trained?"

"It's possible. The Imaiz buys and sells many slaves, using many different auctioneers. Nobody save the prefect would have a continuous record of any single slave's history. Dion-daizan could hold one for years and then return him to the market—and nobody would be the wiser."

"But the auctioneers keep records of their individual transactions?"

"They keep all normal records by way of trade. What did you have in mind?"

"I doubt Di Irons will allow us access to the prefecture records. But I need an individual history for every slave we possess. Go back to the auctioneers and use whatever pressures you must to obtain copies of their records relating to the slaves in whom we're interested. I'll have a computer programmed at the spaceport. With it we should be able to reconstruct individual histories—I want to know of any slave whose bond has been with the *Imaiz* for one year or more."

"With what object?"

"So that we may closely question those whom the *Imaiz* may have trained or influenced. They may tell us much about Dion, his objectives and his facilities. When we've finished we have the legal right to do with them whatever the evidence suggests. We should at least find the men behind the warehouse sabotage. Possibly we'll find many more who've not yet had the time to make a move against us."

Catuul's eyes shone with comprehension. "It's a good plan, friend Tito. I don't anticipate much difficulty about copying the auctioneers' records. It's frequently done by those comparing slave stock for breeding purposes."

"Then the matter is settled," said Ren. "When the director gets back he's going to expect us to have some pretty damaging ammunition aimed at the *Imaiz*. He's not going to be too happy about the loss of the warehouse. Some of the essential oils in it were priceless by any standards. From this point on we're very much at war with the *Imaiz*."

V

Vestevaal, on his return, was much perturbed that the *Imaiz* had struck the first damaging blow in a fight essentially started by Ren. To cover himself Ren outlined his policy for evaluating the slaves and isolating those who had been under the *Imaiz*'s influence. Vestevaal was impressed by the detail, but pointed out that the action was purely defensive. Wars were not won by orderly retreats.

The merchant worlds of Combien and Rance had firmly stressed to Vestevaal the importance of Anharitte as a free port and had backed their stand by donating the battle cruiser now at the spaceport. The Free Trade Security Council had been just as vociferous and had not only pledged unlimited financial backing, but had insisted on sending a professional troubleshooter, Dr. Alek Hardun, as a technical backup for Ren's team. Implicit in this latter action was the threat that if Ren did not make a success of defeating the *Imaiz*, the merchant worlds and the Free Trade Council were quite prepared to move in a stronger cadre to settle the question.

"Nevertheless," said Ren, "if we're to retain the cooperation of the societies, we must first observe the principle of harassment and feud. To attempt outright war on the *Imaiz* at this stage could set even the societies against us, because we're out-worlders and they're indigenous. I know all the arguments, but if we turn public opinion against us the planetary government will have to act—and we'll have lost the free port anyway."

"Well, it's still your show, Tito. But let's see some positive action against the Imaiz. I want to see him hit where it hurts and not only for my personal satisfaction. I have to make reports back to the Free Trade Council. I never was much good at making negative reports."

"Then how about this for an opener? We intend to contest Zinder's bondship with Dion-daizan."

Vestevaal swung around abruptly.

"Damn!" he said. "That would certainly make Dion sit up. How would you set about it?"

Ren smiled wolfishly. "All bondships have to be registered at the prefecture—and that's the only official record. If anything happened to the entry regarding the bondship of Zinder to Dion-daizan, the Imaiz would have no legal way of proving his ownership."

"And it can be arranged that something will happen to the entry?"

"The register clerk is a minor member of the Society of Pointed Tails."

"Surely it isn't as simple as that."

"No. In normal circumstances the loss of the entry would not affect the position, because the rights of ownership of the bond would not be contested. But in this case the ownership will be called into question by the Pointed Tails acting on your behalf. As prefect, Lord Di Irons won't be very happy about the situation, but in order to uphold the law he'll have to impound Zinder until the matter is settled. That leaves Dion-daizan with two courses of action. He can take the case to the supreme court in Gaillen—where he would win, of course, except that the litigation could take a year—"

"Or?"

"He could take the quicker course of accepting the fact that he has no provable right to Zinder's bond. In that case Zinder would be put into the slave market, from which Dion-daizan could hope to buy her back."

"As a very rich man he should have no trouble on that score," said Vestevaal dubiously.

"No. But it's an open market. Anyone can bid who's entitled to hold a slave-bond. That rules you out as a direct participant, but it doesn't stop the Pointed Tails from acting on your behalf. If we bid against Dion, using our backing from the Galactic Bank as guarantee, we could force up the price to where even Dion's resources would be strained. We could make him cripple himself financially in order to save her."

The director smote his knee in lusty approval.

"You know, Tito, you've something of a genius for this sort of thing. Keep up this level of skul-duggery and we'll see you on the Free Trade Council yet."

Heartened, Ren strolled down to the lodge of the Pointed Tails. The place always impressed and fascinated him. Here the ancient *Ahhn* customs and architecture had been carefully preserved from outworld influences. The walls and ceilings of the lodge were ornamented with red and gold reliefs showing stylized pictures of legendary battles, with captions worded in the original but now lapsed High-Ahhn cuneiform script. The whole establishment was richly carpeted, hung with remarkably descriptive tapestries and scented with delicate fragrances. It was the closest the *Ahhn* had ever come to creating a temple. In its halls the history of a proud and intelligent race was set out to show its richness and cohesion and a depth of culture that could have been the envy of many older civilizations.

Catuul Gras seemed to be expecting him and Ren was not surprised. He knew the intimate web of observation and communication with which the societies laced the city.

"Does the director approve of the plan to contest Zinder's bond?" Catuul asked.

"He does. We're to proceed as planned. I think we'd best make our move this afternoon, in case some suspicion of what we intend leaks back to the *Imaiz*."

"I agree, friend Tito. Speed and secrecy are essential. We will watch for Zinder to come to the fruit market today. As soon as I'm sure she's there I'll have my colleague, Mallow Rade, lay formal complaint at the prefecture and demand her impoundment."

"And the entry in the register?"

"That's already taken care of. The matter only waits for us to draw it to the prefect's attention. But news travels with the flies in Anharitte. I suggest neither you nor your director show yourselves outside your chambers until the watchmen have arrested her. I hope the prefect will have enough sense to bring sufficient men to prevent any trouble. As the director's agent, it will be

necessary for you to be present at the formal dis-
cussion of the case afterward. It might be safer if
the director didn't expose himself at all for a day
or two."

"I doubt he'll agree," said Ren. "But I'll try to
get the point over to him. How's the work going
on collecting information for preparing histories
on the slaves?"

"Slowly. As fast as we get the lists complete
we're sending them by runner to Dr. Hardun at the
spaceport."

"Good. Have we any results as yet?"

"Most interestingly, yes. We can't produce the
histories until all the copying is complete, but
already a pattern is starting to emerge. The Imaiz
buys and sells many slaves in an apparently random fashion. But Dr. Hardun's pointed out that
there's a system behind it."

"Oh? What sort of system?" Ren was immediately attentive.

"Dion-daizan has an arrangement with the
slave auctioneers whereby he's notified when a
new batch of slaves is available. He sends his
steward to make a preliminary viewing, then bids
heavily for those he chooses."

"Which is surely a reasonable practice?"

"Yes, except that he purchases many times his
normal labor requirement. All but a few of these
he shortly returns to the market for resale."

"And presumably makes a profit on the deal."

Catuul shook his head. "No. The significant
thing is that he usually takes a loss because he
outbid the market in the first place."

"I don't see—" Ren's voice carried a note of
puzzlement. "Then, assuming he's no philan-

thropist, the value of the transactions must lie uniquely in the few he doesn't return for sale."

Catuul nodded. "The only information we could gain about them was obtained by questioning the ones he rejected. It appears that all the slaves he purchases are given a very thorough medical checkup and put through a series of tests."

"What sort of tests?"

"I think you outworlders describe them as intelligence and aptitude tests. The few who pass remain with the Imaiz. The failures are returned to the market."

"So that Dion-daizan is cultivating a select group of intelligent, capable and healthy slaves?"

"Presumably. But it's interesting to guess at the standards he's working toward. Dr. Hardun examined the best of the latest batch the Imaiz had offered for resale. Some of Dion's rejects were not only above average intelligence and fitness for the slave caste—they were also above average for citizens of any class."

Ren's scowl caused his eyebrows to meet. "So Dion's not only building a select group of slaves, he's culling an elite. Zinder's no happy accident. Nor is she likely to be unique. Damn—how long has this been going on, Catuul?"

"Certainly for ten years, probably longer. I suppose at least seventy per cent of marketable slaves in Anharitte have been through his hands at some time or another. And he also buys some in the provinces."

"And pure-bred Ahhn stock is renowned for its high intelligence. Dion's probably acquired a concentration of brains in Magda that is unique on Roget—perhaps unique on any of the known worlds. Can you arrange that only low-grade slaves are offered to Dion in future?"

"I'll do what I can. With most auctioneers a little pressure will do the trick. The ones we can't influence are those the Pointed Tails themselves are duty-bound to protect. We can't hurt one of our own clients for the benefit of another."

"Then tell them frankly what we think the *Imaiz* is about. Ask for their cooperation. It's in their interests to work with us because if the *Imaiz* wins, the slave trade dies."

"It might work with some," said Catuul dubiously. "But others make much money out of the *Imaiz*. There will be many who won't want to offend him and who will be suspicious of your motives."

VI

Ren stayed at the window of his office chambers all that afternoon. Zinder was late arriving. Finally, however, her dark hair and proud bearing made her as apparent in the crowd as a lantern in the darkness. Even the excellence of her flowing gown set her as a woman apart and made her impossible to miss. Attuned as he was to the pattern of undercurrents in the populace, Ren could sense a tension in the market, as though some suspicion of what was to take place had already passed as rumor.

Vestevaal fretted in a chair behind him. A man of direct action, he had no use for patient observation from behind half-drawn curtains, nor did he accept the principle that feud and harassment were necessary preliminaries to destroying an enemy. Nevertheless he obeyed Ren's insistence that he confine himself indoors at least until after Zinder's arrest. He amused himself by interrogating the spaceport computer complex from Ren's line-fed office terminal and inspecting the agency accounts in the minutest detail.

When the watchmen arrived Ren saw the tension visibly rise in the market. As they moved in the direction of Zinder the scene became tinged with menace almost to the point of open resistance. But Di Irons knew his trade. As the arresting officers moved to take the slave girl, a second force of watchmen was deployed through the crowd ready to nip in the bud any pockets of disobedience. Even so the resentment was building to crisis proportions and some slight catalyst could easily have tipped the balance into violence. Ren understood now Catuul's insistence that Vestevaal should not be present when the arrest took place.

It was Zinder herself, however, who averted the dangerous phase. She shrugged amusedly at the watchmen's advance, then turned and addressed herself to the crowd. Ren could not hear what she said, but he was certain from the attention she was receiving that she was completely in control of the situation. She calmed and pacified the group around her and told it something that proved such a huge joke that those nearest to her broke away laughing and went to retell it to others.

Prefect Di Irons thrust his way through and spoke to her. Again she laughed, and even he came out of the encounter with a reluctant smile curling the corners of his determined mouth. Then Zinder allowed herself to be escorted away. None of the watchmen touched her. They formed a double rank and she, obligingly, walked between them, moving off in the direction of the prefecture. The marketplace relaxed, yet returned not to trade but rather to heated and speculative conversation. Di Irons and the watchmen stood stolidly watchful for any hotheads who might try to rekindle hostility.

When Catuul Gras came up, Ren met him at the door.

"I think it's safe now, friend Tito. I have men enough to cover you to the prefecture. The hearing will take place as soon as Dion-daizan can get a spokesman there. Zinder has predicted to the crowd that the Imaiz will teach the director a great lesson. I must speak with him at once."

"He's inside," said Ren.

"Good. You go along to the prefecture. I'll follow as soon as I can."

Ren buckled on his sword and carefully checked the readiness of the blaster which he wore concealed beneath his shirt. Warily he moved out into the square. Surprisingly, nobody seemed to pay him much attention. This was now the battle of the giants, the Imaiz versus Vestevaal. Ren was merely a bit-player and not a main participant at all.

As he passed out of the square a sudden grip on his arm made Ren swing around. He found himself face to face with the prefect.

"Agent Ren, I'm not deceived. I can read your hand behind this little charade. I don't know what you hope to gain by antagonizing the Imaiz, but let me repeat my warning. Dion is more cunning that you'll allow. Twist his tail too often and he'll break you into a thousand parts. And if your machinations cause public trouble in Anharitte—I'll break you myself. I hope I make myself understood?"

"Perfectly," said Ren. "But I pay well for the best available advisers and they guarantee we're engaged in nothing contrary to the law. I take it we've a perfect right to request that Zinder be impounded pending a legal inquiry?"

"You have that right through a society," agreed Di Irons. "But I would not have thought you well advised to exercise it. The loss of the register entry is in itself suspect. I am now looking for a de-spoiler of prefecture records—and Dion-daizan will be looking for blood. I suspect that if I delay my inquiries a little my problem will be answered for me. Be very cautious, Ren. You've chosen a dangerous adversary."

The prefect moved away. Now that Zinder had actually been removed to the prefecture, the whole area had assumed an atmosphere of disturbed indignation that seemed unlikely to flare more violently. However, it was obvious that only the presence of so many watchmen had prevented a riot and open interference with the arrest. Ren understood how perilously close the incident had been to causing a breach of the peace and he saw that in this the Imaiz had a powerful weapon he could use against the Pointed Tails. By creating a public outcry at a similar maneuver he could easily throw the blame back on to the society and its employer as the prime sources of public unrest.

Ren's arrival at the prefecture was just in time for him to witness the lodging of an official notice contesting the Imaiz's ownership of Zinder by Mallow Rade, a junior scribe of the Pointed Tails. When the paper had been recorded Di Irons, whose mood seemed to be of thunder, called formally for a spokesman from the House of Magda to pose a rebuttal.

For a long time nobody moved. Then, from the back of the crowd, a young slave pushed his way forward and presented his stewardship credentials to Di Irons.

"Ah, Barii." Di Irons seemed slightly relieved. "Do you know how Dion-daizan wishes to proceed in this matter?"

Barii, who bore his slave mark, together with the house symbol of Magda, like a proud badge on his naked arms, nodded. Ren was watching the youth intently, noting the same quiet confidence in the boy he had recognized in Zinder. Here was both an intelligence and a competence that had no place in the slave.

"May I see the register from which Dion's title is missing?"

Di Irons brought out the volume and opened it to the disputed page, exposing the rows of names scrawled painfully in a large and almost illegible script. One of the entries had clearly been over-written at a later date. There was no doubt that the alteration had been deliberate.

Barii reached into his pouch and drew out some article the purpose of which was not plain until the unexpected brilliance of an electronic flash glared back from the yellowing pages. A second flash illuminated the startled face of the register clerk. Barii put his camera back into its pouch and bowed to Di Irons. If his face held any expression at all it was one of concealed amusement and anticipation.

Then Barii spoke.

"Dion-daizan has noted the objections to his ownership of Zinder's bond. Everyone in Anharitte knows that Zinder's preeminence is largely due to her association with the House of Magda—thus there can be no doubt of the true tenure of her bond. However, the Imaiz is immensely concerned about the maintenance of the law on the three hills. In consequence he has directed that, since no clear title to his ownership seems to be recorded in the prefecture, he will

renounce his claim to being Zinder's legal bond-
holder. He requests that the slave in question be
put to public auction and that the proceeds of the
sale be dedicated to the public funds of the city, as
is the custom."

Di Irons had listened to this speech with growing disbelief. He seemed about to throw in some
crushing protest, but was stopped by something
he saw in Barii's face. The prefect's shrug was
massive and uncomprehending.

"So be it," he said. "It's the considered opnion
of the prefecture that the bondship of Zinder has
no clear tenure. The slave woman called Zinder
will therefore be returned to the market and sub-
mitted to public auction. Let it be known that
anyone desirous of obtaining this property may
attend tomorrow at the preset hour and bid legal
coinage for unrestricted bond rights. The matter
is now dismissed from these courts."

Ren's attentive eyes fell upon the register clerk,
whose hands had undoubtedly been responsible
for the alteration of the entry. The clerk seemed
relieved that Di Irons had so easily acceded to the
contesting of the records, yet his nervous glances
at Barii showed that he knew retribution was still
due. The steward's act of photographing the entry
had shaken him badly and his ashen hue was
indicative of a deep and mortal fear. Knowing of
the clerk's association with the Pointed Tails, Ren
was pleased to note that members of the clan
moved protectively nearer to the clerk to guard
him against danger.

Di Irons was looking at his treacherous clerk
with something akin to murder in his eyes. His
sword hand convulsively gripped the hilt of his

weapon. For a moment Ren thought that Di Irons
was going to attack the fellow, but Barii moved
between them and a slight lift of his eyebrows
caused the prefect to relax.

Ren relaxed too.

All Anharitte was watching the outcome of this
dispute—the supposed omnipotence on the *Imaiz*
was now on public trial. Dion-daizan's easy ac-
quiescence to the challenge might mean only that
he had chosen the slave market as the quicker
route for regaining Zinder's bond, but currently
the wizard's public image must have suffered a
lowering as a result of Ren's audacious move. Ren
had well prepared the ground ahead. It was going
to be an interesting battle.

Ren awoke in the night with a start. A house
servant was shaking his arm.

"Agent Ren—wake up, please! The prefect
sends for you urgently."

Shaking the sleep from his head, Ren roused
himself and forced his mind to concentrate.

"What did you say?"

"The prefect sends watchmen to guide you. The
register clerk is dead."

"Damn!" said Ren, struggling into his clothes.
"What has it to do with me?"

He went downstairs to remonstrate with the
watchmen who waited in the downstairs office.
The sergeant listened to his protest without expression.

"The Lord Di Irons is aware of your position.
Nonetheless he directs we conduct you to the
place of the accident."

"Accident?"

The sergeant refused to be drawn out. "Come, Agent Ren. Lord Di Irons himself will explain the matter."

Ren reached for his cloak, girded on his sword and reluctantly followed the watchmen into the night.

The air outside was chill and damp with the clinging mists from the sea. The whole township was in darkness save for the occasional flare of the watch braziers and the torches carried by his escort. The sudden transition from sleep to the cold darkness and the leaping flames of the brands touched the scene with unreality made only more credible by the hardness of the shifting, round cobbles underneath his feet.

The route the watchmen chose was unfamiliar to Ren, involving numerous turns down narrow streets and alleys until his whole sense of direction was destroyed. Finally the party halted in front of a mean drinking place and Ren waited impatiently while the watchmen knocked on a small and unfamiliar door. Shortly, bolts were drawn and the great bulk of Di Irons himself loomed between the door posts.

"Ah, Ren. Come in. You're an astute man, so I'm going to give you an opportunity to exercise your cleverness."

The prefect leaned past Ren and instructed the watchmen to continue searching the area. Then he withdrew into the room and beckoned to Ren. The doorway was so small that even Ren had to duck his head as he entered. The ceiling inside was scarecely higher and the room stank of cheap alcohol and the presence of too many bodies. Ten of the Pointed Tails, Catuul Gras among them, sat in a circle around a flickering lamp, looking uneasily at Di Irons. On the far side of the room another door led out to a small brick courtyard, which two watchmen illuminated with poled lanterns. Across the threshold of this second door lay the register clerk. He had a fatal wound in his throat and blood spread wide across the floor.

Di Irons was crushing. "I lay the responsibility for this piece of mischief at your door, Ren."

The statement caught Ren completely off guard.

"Mine?"

"Of course."

"But I had nothing whatever to do with his death."

"Then you should consider better the consequences of your actions. I know perfectly well that this man overwrote Dion-daizan's title in the register and I know that your money induced him to do it. Now he's dead because of it. If this piece of bloodshed is an example of how you mean to harass the Imaiz, you'd be well advised to employ a more competent society." He spat in the general direction of Catuul Gras.

"I admit I could have been an interested party," said Ren. "But if the man's dead it was the Imaiz who had him killed. Why don't you tax him with it?"

"I would—if I had a shred of proof. But we've found no trace of an assassin, no sign of any weapon. It's only our suspicion that the Imaiz would want this man destroyed. There's no tangible connection with Dion-daizan. If you can give me proof of his complicity, I'll take the issue to his door. Until then I regard this as the result of your own inept machinations."

"You've found no weapon?" Ren was

perplexed. He turned to Catuul Gras. "Weren't you here when it happened?"

"I was—we all were." Catuul's gesture encompassed his comrades. "We chose this house because it has only one door connecting with the street—and that door could be stoutly bolted. The windows have shutters inside and the courtyard leads only to blank walls. Here, at least, we thought we could defend him from the mighty wrath of the *Imaiz*."

"Then what happened?" Ren was impatient.

"We were drinking moderately and talking and because the roof is low the room soon grew hot. We opened the door to the courtyard to let in air, since we dared not unbar the windows. Even then, for safety's sake, we put three men in the courtyard so that no surprise attack could come from there."

"And?"

"The clerk was badly worried and drank more freely than was wise. Knowing the courtyard was guarded, he felt safe in going to the door to relieve himself into the gully. As he reached the door he seemed to choke and we saw him fall down just where you see him now. His throat was torn and he drowned in his own blood."

"Then how did—?"

"We don't know. Those in the courtyard saw and heard nothing, nor did those of us who stayed inside. Whatever split his throat has not been found, though we've searched the yard and the room a dozen times. No man among us has recent blood on his weapons, so even treachery is ruled out. I personally think that the *Imaiz* sent an invisible beast to claw out his throat."

"You know I can't accept that," said Ren angrily. "There are no such things as invisible beasts."

Ren bent down to examine the wound, but realized, with his fingers and shoes slipping with blood, that he had neither the knowledge nor the stomach to gain much from the examination. He passed on out into the courtyard, inspected its solid walls and tried to scrutinize the higher surroundings, which were obscured by darkness. Finding no solution to the mystery, he climbed back past the body in the doorway and faced Di Irons.

"If you'll permit, Prefect, I'd like Dr. Hardun at the spaceport to perform an examination of the body."

"Will that help, Agent Ren? The man is dead—his throat is gone. What more can be learned from him?"

"There must be some evidence of whatever broke his throat. We've many facilities on the battle cruiser. A weapon that caused that damage must have left a trace. If it's there we'll find it."

The prefect shrugged. "I see no harm in your trying. If you wish you may come and take the body after daybreak. And you, Catuul, will have an accounting to make to his widow. I shall hold the Pointed Tails responsible for the cremation and all expenses. Nobody's lightly going to disturb the peace while I'm prefect on the three hills."

"It will be as you direct, Prefect," said Catuul Gras quietly, though a variety of emotions struggled in his voice.

The prefect called his watchmen and departed. Ren turned to Catuul in anger.

"The fate of the clerk is unfortunate, but I thought your society could have handled a thing like the death of a member with discretion. How did Di Irons come to learn of it?"

"I asked myself the same thing," said Catuul. "The watchmen claim they were called here because of complaints of a disturbance. But there was no disturbance. When the man fell dead we were too amazed to cry out—and thereafter we were too afraid of attracting attention. Yet the watchmen arrived within minutes of the death. Indeed, they must have started on their way while the man was still alive. Whoever complained to them must have done so with a foreknowledge of the death to come."

"Di Irons seems reluctant to agree that the Imaiz must have been responsible. Does he have some sympathy for Dion-daizan?"

"I think not. Di Irons concerns himself with the peace of the city. If two sides feud, he cares little which side goes under—as long as the fighting is contained. Knowing this, Dion is perhaps using him to harass us like fools. I swear to you one thing, friend Tito—if Dion-daizan hopes to buy Zinder back at the auction, he'll find her the most expensive purchase he has ever attempted."

VII

The slave market was situated on the eastern slopes of Anharitte, in the bowl through which descended the old road leading to the valley and to Secondhill and T'Ampere. The location was said to have been chosen in the days when slaves were leased to merchant vessels entering the shipping lanes to trade their cargoes along the inland rivers and canals. The slaves were used to handle the cargo exchanges and in theory returned to their owners when the ships once again reached the Aprillo *en route* to the sea.

However, so many slaves were lost through misuse by their temporary masters that the system fell into disrepute and slave-leases were abandoned.

It was doubtful if a more astute class of man existed on all the three hills than the average slave auctioneer. Operating usually on a percentage basis against the immutable laws of supply and demand, he knew well how to present his wares to the best advantage and how to drive the shrewdest bargain.

This afternoon, however, most of the sale rostrums were unattended by clients, no matter how eloquently the vendors phrased their sales address. A curious order had replaced the normal hubbub of the slave market and almost all the onlookers were facing a solitary platform high on the slope. Watchmen were in abundance, as if to emphasize the weight of the hand of the law, but the crowd was genuinely good humored and interested in the coming spectacle. The atmosphere was one of anticipation rather than resentment. The occasion was the sale of Zinder's bond—and speculation had it that the *Imaiz* himself would be coming to the bidding.

Ren had arrived early with Catuul Gras and a more than nominal bodyguard of Pointed Tails. They first approached the auctioneer to establish Catuul's right to bid on behalf of Magno Vestevaal and to offer proof of the considerable funding on which they could draw if necessity arose. Then, under the jovial eyes of the happy auctioneer, they were offered selected seating in front of the rostrum from which to conduct their business. At a few minutes to the preset hour at which the proceedings should have begun there was still no sign of anyone from the House of Magda. Then the crowd divided abruptly and a man strode through alone—Dion-daizan, the wizard of Anharitte.

This was the first time that Tito Ren had ever been really close to the *Imaiz* and he studied Dion carefully as the latter spoke to the auctioneer in the customary mode of introduction. Ren's analysis did not leave him particularly impressed. Of indeterminate age, though probably nearing fifty years, Dion appeared to eschew all forms of showmanship or affectation.

Clad in a simple white gown, without apparent weapons, Dion's face was neither distinguished nor particularly memorable. Only the movement of his hands indicated quiet confidence and competence that warned the agent to be wary. Whether or not the man was a Terran was not discernible from his unexceptional appearance, but he was obviously skilled in the control both of himself and others. And from the respect with which he was treated it was obvious that he was nearly a god in the eyes of Anharitte.

The auctioneer held up his hands for attention. His prologue was treated to a quantity of good-natured banter from the onlooking assembly, but this died when Zinder herself was brought out.

Ren was stunned. He had seen the work of beauticians on seven prime worlds, but never in all his experience had he seen such exquisite presentation of the female form as Zinder managed on her way to the rostrum. The audience of perhaps a thousand held its breath as she walked on stage in burnished radiance. Only Dion himself seemed unimpressed.

Even the auctioneer became speechless. Though he had issued instructions that Zinder be readied for the market, he had not anticipated the skill in the hands of several inhabitants of Magda whose task it had somehow become. He started to make his customary appeal to would-be purchasers, but seemed to become awed by the wonder of it all. Evidently lost for words, he finally paid her the ultimate tribute—he kneeled and kissed her hand.

A cheer rose from the assembly.

Catuul Gras came coldly to his feet. "I bid you five barr for the bond," he said.

So low a price was a calculated insult. The

audience tensed with anticipation. It was going to
be an evening to remember.

"Raised to the second power," said Dion-
daizan unhurriedly.

"Six barr to the second power," said Catuul
Gras. He was playing his hand narrowly.

"To the third power," said Dion-daizon.

"Seven to the third power," Catuul said.

Ren, whose mathematical training probably
transcended that of any in the watching public,
lapsed into mental calculation of the true value of
the bids, unsettled by the way in which the Imaiz
each time multiplied the value of the bid by raising the index. It was absolutely certain that at
some point the Imaiz was going to approach a
figure he could not possibly afford, and at that
point Catuul must withdraw. He was relieved to
note that as the values rose, the scribe became
more punctilious about obtaining confirmation
before proceeding.

Nevertheless, Ren continued disconcerted by
the actions of the Imaiz, who seemed determined
to drive the price into truly astronomical figures.

It said much for the mental constitution of the
auctioneer that he was able to continue function-
ing as evenly as he did in the face of the rapidly
mounting values. He was sweating profusely and
developed a marked tremor of the limbs when his
due commission on the sale would have made
him rich beyond all his dreams. Still the contest
continued.

Ren was now using a pocket calculator to bring
out the absolute values of the bids in terms of the
galactic credits. The Imaiz used no calculating
aids, but Ren had the feeling that Dion-daizan was
nevertheless completely aware of the real value of

the figures with which they were playing. Only Catuul seemed out of his depth and repeatedly looked at Ren for confirmation that he was intended to continue.

"Ten barrs raised to the sixth power," said Catuul uneasily. This was more money than he had ever heard of.

"Ten to the seventh power." Dion-daizon showed slight signs of agitation although Ren suspected the wizard was well within his ample budget.

"Eleven to the seventh."

The Imaiz faltered and a gasp of anticipation ran through the watching crowd. Ren felt a savage elation at the thought of having placed the Imaiz on public trial. It was a beautiful piece of harassment.

"Eleven barrs to the eighth power," said the Imaiz finally.

Somebody in the crowd with some appreciation of the amount involved gave him a round of applause. Ren signaled for Catuul to continue.

"Twelve to the eighth," said Catuul grimly.

The Imaiz stopped and scanned the crowd, as if trying to estimate the cost of losing face. Then he shrugged resignedly and turned again to the auctioneer. Ren still judged Dion-daizan to be within the limits of his purse, but the wizard was obviously struggling with considerations that evidently weighed as heavily with him as the regaining of Zinder.

"Twelve to the ninth," said the master of Magda in a voice that could scarcely be heard.

Catuul Gras stole a warning look at Ren, but the agent had a reasonable idea of the Imaiz's true financial potential, based on the yearly spaceport dues paid to the House of Magda. He knew it was possible to squeeze the *Imaiz* even drier.

"Thirteen to the ninth," said Catuul.

"Thirteen to the tenth," said the Imaiz, his voice suddenly sharp with a new resolve.

"What's the old fox up to?" asked Catuul anxiously. "Has he really got that much money?"

"I think he has. But he's becoming uncomfortable. I think just once more must take him to the limit."

"Fourteen to the tenth," said Catuul.

The auctioneer had long since ceased to comprehend the magnitude of the figures being used and cared only that each bid was higher than the last. On a commission of even one per cent his family would be rich for generations.

Dion-daizan sat, his face suddenly bland. The auctioneer looked at him questioningly.

"Dion—don't you wish to raise?"

"Of course not." The *Imaiz's* face was alive with humor, revealing a richness of personality he had hitherto concealed. "Believe me, it's not through lack of finance, but in observance of a principle."

"Principle?" The auctioneer was lost.

"Yes," said Dion-daizan happily. "Anyone who would bid fourteen to the tenth power barrs for Zinder must have achieved a true appreciation of her worth. Far be it from me to deter such enlightenment. It's not every day that my progressive policies gain such eminent recognition. Nor is it often in Anharitte that the real worth of a human being is so openly acknowledged. May others soon become as wise as Director Vestevaal."

Ren watched with mounting horror as the hammer fell. The auctioneer's voice boomed above the murmur of the crowd.

"I hereby declare the slave Zinder to be sold to the Society of Pointed Tails acting on behalf of its client, Director Magno Vestevaal. The agreed price is fourteen barrs raised to the tenth power—a completely unprecedented sum for any slave at any time in history and a truly magnificent tribute to the slave-training policy of the House of Magda."

"Damn!" Ren, ashen of face, staggered to his feet. It was too late to rescind the bid—the transaction was already complete. He turned appealingly to Catuul Gras.

"What the hell's Dion up to?"

"Teaching the director a lesson, I should think," said Catuul grimly. "Well he's certainly made his point—and at our expense. Let's face it, Tito. He's beaten us at our own game."

"I don't believe it," said Ren, consumed by his own anger. "A man like Dion isn't going to let Zinder go."

Zinder, from the rostrum, had displayed a keen interest in the proceedings. Far from seeming betrayed by Dion-daizan's action, she appeared elated. She saluted her late master who, in turn, approached her to kiss her hand. Then Dion-daizan turned to the crowd and raised his hands in an expansive gesture of triumph. The ensuing cheer was probably the loudest roar of acclamation from human throats that Roget had ever known.

The auctioneer took Zinder's halter and led her, a symbol of apparent meekness, to Catuul Gras.

The latter took the plaited rope as though it were likely to grow hot and looked somewhat stupidly at Ren.

"The sale price is on guarantee from the Galactic Bank," said the auctioneer. "The contract settlement is now between the purchaser and the city administration. Therefore I have no need to detain you, except to remind you of the convention that the title of the bond must be registered at the prefecture within seven hours or the money is forfeit and the bond is returned to the city administration."

"I understand," said Catuul Gras. "I assure you the bond will be duly registered within the time."

Ren said nothing, not being able to trust himself to speak. Having been tricked into authorizing such an astronomical sum on the acquisition of a single female slave, he knew that the blackest hour of his career was upon him. An error in his judgment had caused this embarrassment to happen. He had been certain above all things that the *Imaiz* would not allow Zinder to be bought over his head. Now the wizard was standing both pleased and apparently unworried as Zinder was led away by the hands of his sworn enemies. Ren was still not convinced that the *Imaiz* would allow it to happen, but failed to see how he could prevent it—unless by some ambush or deception Dion managed to stop the bond's being registered in time.

Catuul's mind was apparently working along the same lines. He signaled members of his clan out from the crowd and sent them ahead to see that the roads Zinder and her new owners had to travel were free from possible trouble. With practiced inconspicuousness the little group melted away.

"I think," said Catuul, "that we had best pick up the director and get the registration over as soon as possible. That is—" he glanced uneasily at the radiant Zinder—"assuming that you wish to go through with it."

"For that sort of money," said Ren ruefully, "the deal had better be legally complete. Though the devil knows how it's going to look on the account books." Despite the immensity of his blunder the humor of the situation overwhelmed him and he started to chuckle spasmodically at his own discomfort.

The assembled crowd was beginning to disperse with much laughter and amused speculation. Not a few came to have a closer look at Zinder wearing the customary bondage halter. For a moment Ren felt angered by what he regarded as morbid curiosity. But when he saw the proud and dominant strength in Zinder's face, he realized that on the end of the halter was a powerful social catalyst. What he was parading through the streets was the anachronistic shame of Anharitte's slave trade. He and the Pointed Tails were being used to underscore the unfairness and absurdity of the system. While he was agent for the titular master, it was obviously the slave who held command of the situation and the hearts of the onlookers.

Thinking deeply in this vein, Ren walked ahead. Catuul followed, leading Zinder on the halter as if she were any common beast. Four of the Pointed Tails armsmen acted as a guard detail and also carried the torches, which were just needing to be lit as the purple dusk closed down. Ren found the journey acutely embarrassing. His civilized instincts prompted him to make conversation with Zinder, whose intellectual talents were probably more than equal to his own. But the halter she wore about her neck made such an action seem incongruous and he could think of no topic of conversation that could span the dual standards that had been thrust upon him.

He therefore stalked ahead of the group, growing increasingly angry at his own inability to resolve the conflict within himself. He sensed in the situation the ingenuity of the *Imaiz* in attacking the slave problem in this particular way and his respect for the wizard increased considerably. The *Imaiz* was forming a schism not only in society but also deep in the psyches of individual participants—such as himself. It was a dangerous and powerful game, and Ren knew that if Diondaizan were not stopped he would ultimately win the battle.

Magno Vestevaal was waiting in Ren's chambers. The director had been drinking liberally, presumably celebrating a victory that had not been won. Ren roused him from his chair, knowing the worst had best be told without delay.

"We have to go immediately to the prefecture to register the bond."

"Register?" Vestevaal's eyes refocused on Ren in an instant. "What the hell do you mean?"

"I mean that the *Imaiz* played with us as he might with fools. You now own Zinder."

"Own Zinder?" Vestevaal appeared to sober himself by a tremendous effort of will. "I see! And how much did this—ah—acquisition cost us, Tito?"

"Fourteen barrs to the tenth power," said Ren, being deliberately obtuse to soften the shock.

"What in hell is that in terms of money?"

Ren bent over his office calculator and converted the figures first to duodecimal galactic credits and then to the Terran ten-based notation which the director handled more happily. Vestevaal watched him steadily, sensing in Ren's actions a certain reticence that foretold of trouble.

"Well?"

Ren had finished the calculations and was examining the printout, wondering how to present it in the best light.

"You'd better sit down again," he said. "Would you believe about two hundred million million Solar dollars?"

For a moment the director appeared in danger of suffering a seizure. At last he swore. "You could buy two battle cruisers for less. Tito—have you any idea how I'm going to explain that sort of expenditure to the Free Trade Council? What are you trying to do—ruin me?"

"No, but I think it's a reasonable certainty that the Imaiz is. He promised to teach you a lesson. I guess this is it. But I still think we've hit him where it hurts. After all, we've got Zinder."

"Where is she?" asked Vestevaal. The color was slowly coming back into his cheeks. "Do you have her?"

"She's outside with Catuul and the guard."

"Then fetch her in—fetch her in! Where's your hospitality, Tito? It's not every day you get the chance to entertain somebody who's worth more than all your Company executives rolled into one.

Ren called for Zinder. Unlike Ren, Magno Vestevaal was in no doubt as to how she should be
treated. He borrowed Ren's sword to cut the halter
from her neck, then handed her into a chair as
though she were a queen. She took the incident
completely unabashed. Already she seemed to
have established with Vestevaal a degree of rap-
port that reached to depths Ren could not envi-
sion. She accepted wine and fell into a quiet conversation with the director until Ren was forced to
interrupt, fearing that if they further delayed they
would become overdue for registering her bond.

The remainder of the journey to the prefecture
was in marked contrast with that from the slave
market. Magno Vestevaal led the way, engaged in
earnest conversation with the slave girl on his
arm, while Ren and Catuul followed disconso-
lately at their heels. The four armsmen had dispersed themselves fore and aft of the group,
swords drawn and ready for trouble, since Catuul
still feared an ambush or an interference designed
to delay the registration of the bond. The director,
however, ridiculed the idea of potential trouble
and refused even to remain consistently within
the shield of guards. He was right—inasmuch as
they arrived at the grim portals of the prefecture
without any sign of unwanted intervention.

VIII

The prefecture was bustling with people. Watchmen were returning or departing on duty—clerks were fetching and carrying their massive volumes and a small mob around the slave registry was presumably waiting to see the registration of Zinder. Ren was not surprised to see Barii, the *Imaiz*'s slave-caste steward in the group—and Dion-daizan himself. Everyone turned to watch as the director and his costly prize came across the threshold.

Dion-daizan made a bow of courtesy to Magno Vestevaal, which the latter good-humoredly returned. The director seemed in remarkably good spirits, having regained his equilibrium completely after his shock of learning of Ren's transaction. His reaction to Dion-daizan was an acknowledgment of the excellence of his adversary. Dion's respect was no less evident. Both men turned to regard Zinder, who stood peacock-proud watching the register clerk intently as he painstakingly wrote the details of her bondage on a new page of his mammoth book.

Di Irons came out of his office and took charge of the proceedings. His manner suggested that it was important for the peace of the city that the registration went smoothly. The prefect inspected the entry carefully, held it up for Dion-daizan to examine, then called for the mark of the auctioneer to authenticate the sale.

Catuul went suddenly tense. He had momentarily lost sight of Barii, but finally located him standing behind the *Imaiz*, who had retired discreetly to the rear. Like Ren, the scribe had the gravest doubts that the *Imaiz* would permit the registration to be completed, but it was difficult to see how he could now prevent its finalization. Everyone in the room felt the tension rise and additional watchmen came out from some dark antechamber to stand silent and ready for trouble.

After the auctioneer had made his mark several statutory witnesses followed—Mallow Rade came to sign on behalf of the Pointed Tails. It was then Vestevaal's turn to sign as the ultimate purchaser. Such a succession of names was not usually required, but Di Irons was taking no chances. Necessity demanded that this was one registration that could never be disputed.

Vestevaal was aware that he could be altering the course of history on Roget as he took out his pen. He was buying a legend for hard cash, and the implication of the completed deal was that even enlightenment had its price. This was not, he reflected ruefully, the first time nor was Roget the first world on which that lesson had been learned. As he turned from the book he could not resist flashing a look of triumph in the direction of Dion-daizan. In return he received a polite smile, which might have signified resignation—but probably did not.

The director turned and held out his hand, indicating that Zinder should walk before him. Then a gasp of amazement from the onlookers diverted his attention back to the register. To his astonishment he saw the lines of ink begin to smoke and spread out, charring the surrounding paper. Some potent chemical reaction caused a glow that quickly became a flame that ran up the angled page—and though Vestevaal seized another volume and beat upon the burning book, he succeeded only in completely breaking up the fragile ash, which further disintegrated of its own volition.

All eyes turned accusingly to the *Imaiz*, then back to Di Irons, wondering how the situation was going to be resolved. The prefect, a cloud of smoke still about his startled head, growled in a voice like thunder and savagely pulled the book toward him as he brushed away the burned edges.

"Dion-daizan—I take it this is some work of yours."

"Mine?" The *Imaiz* sounded shocked. "There are ten good people between myself and the book—and have been all evening. Likewise, my servant Barii has not approached the proceedings. I could have had no more to do with the loss of the entry than—say—Agent Ren had with the loss of the title I once owned."

"You make a good point," said Di Irons, glancing sourly at Ren, who had come forward to examine the burned page of the register. "The question is, what's to be done now?"

"Who claims the title to Zinder?" asked the *Imaiz*. His voice, though soft, carried perfectly.

"I do, of course," said Vestevaal.

"Then I contest your title to the bond. I submit that at this moment you can no more prove your ownership than could I a short while after Zinder was taken from me."

"There must have been a thousand witnesses to my purchase tonight." Vestevaal was adamant. "I demand that the registration begin anew."

"You have a thousand witnesses, but all Anharitte knew for ten years that Zinder belonged to me. Whose evidence is the stronger?"

"Stop this!" thundered Di Irons. "Dion, I shall have many words to say to you concerning your conduct this night. And you, Director, and your puppet Ren, are beginning to tire my patience. In the circumstances—I can see that the Imaiz has a valid point. Your situation is no different from his a little while ago. If justice is to be done I think the case should be treated in the same way."

"What does that mean?" asked Vestevaal sharply.

"If you wish, Director, your society can contest my decision in the supreme court at Gaillen. I advise you now that it would be a waste of time to do so, with the Imaiz so closely attentive to his own claims. But my own ruling is this: it's the considered opinion of the prefecture that the bondship of Zinder still has no clear tenure. Under the law it is therefore my duty to impound the slave girl in question and return her to the market for public auction. I have no more to say on the subject."

"But I have," said Vestevaal angrily. "I've paid a great sum of money for that girl. Do I not get that back?"

"What? You squeal because your agents forced a bad bargain?" Di Irons was cuttingly acid. "Come now! As a merchant you're fully aware that all purchases in Anharitte are on the basis of *caveat emptor*—let the purchaser beware. Ren was warned by myself most specifically not to proceed with the gambit. And I'm sure your reputation for trade on this planet would be little helped by your continuing such a claim. Especially—" he leaned forward heavily—"since the money was provided by the Free Trade Council for the express purpose of causing civil mischief in Anharitte. Do you care to take that matter to court, Director? I doubt the planetary government would view the proceedings with much favor."

Vestevaal appeared on the verge of making a critically harsh reply. Then he looked at Zinder. She met his gaze with level inquiry, as if searching for something she expected to find in him. Vestevaal reacted with sudden resolution—a smile of tired humor lit his face.

"My apologies, Prefect. I spoke out of turn. Of course I respect your ruling on both counts. Never let it be said that Magno Vestevaal doesn't know how to accept defeat with dignity."

Vestevaal turned to Zinder and kissed her hand, then bowed to Dion-daizan. He turned to Ren and Catuul Gras and indicated that they all should leave.

"Well, Tito—how's that for being outclassed?" Vestevaal's voice held a note of genuine appreciation. "I've seen some rank skulduggery among the Free Traders, but believe me, Dion-daizan makes the rest of them look like amateurs. Damn it—I'd love to see him on the council!"

"Are we going to take the debt for Zinder without fighting?" asked Ren.

"We have no alternative. We dare not go to court lest we sour the attitude of the planetary government toward Free Trade. You know how parochial these hickworld governments can be."

"This makes me wonder if there's collusion between the Imaiz and the prefect."

"I don't think so. Di Irons is the straightest man I've ever come across. But he's trying to use unsophisticated laws to control a situation with which even sophisticated laws would find it difficult to cope. So he compensates by applying a good measure of rough horse-sense. And why shouldn't he? It's just that sort of approach that keeps Anharitte the place it is. And at least he's helped to cut our losses."

"I don't follow that."

Vestevaal laughed heartily and clapped Ren on the back.

"My dear Tito, you're too damn sober. Don't you realize that without Zinder we've one less mouth to feed and back to clothe? And there's a further problem you haven't even thought of. Suppose we had retained her—what the hell would we have found to do with her?"

The following day Zinder was again put up for sale. The Imaiz took up the bidding and this time nobody opposed him. The hammer fell at the price of one barr. And this was perhaps the final irony.

IX

In the laboratory aboard the battle cruiser at the spaceport Dr. Alek Hardun had been forming his own impressions of the *Imaiz*.

"I'm afraid," he said to Ren, "we're up against a pretty formidable technician."

"You have some answers, Alek?"

"Some. But they reveal a class of technology I had not expected to find on a backward world like this."

Ren sat atop one of the laboratory stools. "Don't worry about the location. I'm already quite convinced that the *Imaiz* is a Terran and is capable of anything including outmanipulating Magno Vestevaal himself. The incident with Zinder could have been funny if it hadn't been so expensive."

Hardun's eyes twinkled momentarily. "I gather it was rather a warm evening," he said. "But all things taken together, I'm not surprised. The way the register clerk died was no less clever."

"Have you found how it was done?"

"Yes. We did a post-mortem examination, but nearly missed the point. We were looking for a projectile of some sort in the esophagus. Of course we didn't find one—rather, we did find it but failed to recognize it for what it was."

"Spare me the riddles," said Ren. "I've been up half the night helping the director to drown his sorrows."

"The answer, my dear Tito, was blood."

"I don't see—"

"Neither did we—at first. But trying to explore all possible avenues we ran some blood analyses to see if anything unusual showed up. Something did. We found two distinct blood groups. One was the blood group of the clerk. The second was undoubtedly human blood but of a completely different group. Working on the second type of blood alone, we were able to determine that it had been carefully processed and then frozen.

"The rest is conjecture, but it's a reasonable supposition that what killed the clerk was a shaft of frozen blood projected by some high velocity instrument at a fairly short range. Such a projectile in the throat would, of course, pass almost unnoticed amid the blood and fragmentation caused by its impact and very shortly it would melt in the warm blood of its victim. A rather neat, self-obscuring murder weapon, I think."

Ren nodded thoughtfully. "And not one likely to be detectable by Di Irons and his primitive police methods. What sort of weapon could have been used to throw a shaft of frozen blood with the necessary velocity?"

Alek Hardun pursed his lips. "That's difficult to say. At first we thought in terms of an air rifle, but your fellow, Catuul Gras, was positive that he and his friends heard no sound at all. I think now that some form of crossbow is more likely. A good one can give you velocity and accuracy not much inferior to a rifle's. The only special requirement is that the bolt must be maintained in a frozen condition until immediately before firing. This presupposes somebody with a Dewar flask and some experience in producing and handling materials at low temperatures. It all ties in neatly with your liquid-oxygen fire at the warehouse. I would not have believed it if I hadn't seen the evidence—but there must be a competent cryogenics man at work in Magda."

"I can't imagine our being able to use your evidence to convince Di Irons," said Ren. "His world is bounded by the four elements—earth, air, fire and water. I don't think the distinction between cryogenics and necromancy is sufficiently obvious to make him move against Diondaizan. Especially when Dion can set a sheet of paper afire at thirty paces without even moving."

"But he didn't," said Hardun. "The director set that afire himself."

"Explain it to me."

"It's another example of the technology I hadn't expected to find. We've been working on the fragments of the page you gave us—and it isn't a paper at all. Somebody had inserted a special page in that book. Certainly the sheet was a fibrous cellulose material, but it had been impregnated with some strong oxidizing compound. Frankly, it would have crumbled to dust in a few weeks anyway, assuming that nobody had even touched it. But it was the ink in the director's pen that touched off the fast reaction."

"But all the others wrote on it without effect," objected Ren.

"True. But on Roget all the available inks are water-based—and I'd be willing to bet the others all used an old-fashioned wet-dip nib pen."

Ren thought back carefully. "I think you're right."

"Well, the effect of a water-based ink on the sheet is negligible. It redistributes the oxidant, but doesn't react with it. But the director predictably signed with his own pen—and that contained a modern outworld organic-based ink. The organics were rapidly oxidized and produced almost spontaneous combustion. The local heat thus liberated was sufficient to touch the rest of the page off in a self-destructive mode. That bond entry was definitely designed to have no future."

Ren smiled ruefully. "I suppose you could say we've only ourselves to blame. We did the same thing to Dion-daizan—but with only a fraction of the subtlety. The devil alone knows how much support he's gained from the incident. I'd guess all Anharitte is laughing at us this morning."

"I think," said Hardun, "you're taking completely the wrong approach. You're making a game of this instead of trying for a fast, decisive strike. I know it's your war, but the problem of the Imaiz is also within my competence. I'd tackle the whole affair quite differently."

"This morning I could use a few ideas. I don't promise to agree, but I'd like to hear your version of how it should be done."

"Not how it should be done," said Hardun. "How it must be done. I was thinking more on the lines of dusting the Castle Magda with carcinogens—or the careful application of nerve gas. Perhaps even the introduction of an ergot derivative into their drinking water—"

Castle Di Guaard was a daunting prospect. Constructed originally as the first defense fortress overlooking the broad Aprillo river, it had seen much service against the Tyrene pirates who ventured to pass under its cannon to reach the internal waterways leading to the soft underflesh of the city and the provinces beyond. The pirates were gone now—their impetus having retreated into the more profitable enterprises of respectable trading houses—but the guns and the grim, crenelated battlements of Castle Di Guaard remained unchanged as though caught in some eddy of time itself.

Matching its image as a fortress was the preparedness of the soldiery contained within its gray stone confines. Indeed, a full lookout and guard were maintained on all walls as though in anticipation of an imminent attack. As Ren was admitted by Sonel Taw, the castellan—or governor—of the castle, he was immediately conscious of being in an armed citadel and, more surprisingly, one in which the men at arms not only carried prime muskets, but seemed fully prepared to use them on the slightest provocation.

The unchanged character of Di Guaard also extended to the slaves, who in the main were ragged, wretched and nervously watchful, as though their lives depended on the speed with which they responded to a call for service. Many of them bore the scars of barbarous punishments—all wore the hangdog expression of whipped curs, which turned Ren's stomach slightly. Nowhere else in Anharitte had he seen slaves reduced to this condition. Remembering the proud strengths of Zinder, he experienced a slight twinge of conscience that his mission to Di Guaard was to gain support for the destruction of the House of Magda.

Castle Di Guaard was built on the principle of a

bailey within a bailey, the outer containing slave quarters, stores and work yards, the inner housing the soldiery. Both were surrounded by the great walls whose machicolated parapets and mural flanking towers were designed to resist attack from any point of the compass. There was no moat, the castle being on two sides met by the sheer drop of the cliffs overhanging the Aprillo delta. The two great gates inland were amply overseen by formidable gatehouses, each with outworks in the form of separate barbican towers.

Ren followed the castellan without comment—and the latter seemed disinclined to enter conversation. At one corner of the inner bailey stood the mighty roundtower of the great keep—the home of Delph Di Guaard himself— and it was here that Ren was led. The tower's broad, flat roof was said to be the highest point in all the provinces and formed an excellent platform for observation and for the light chain-throwing cannon of which Di Guaard seemed inordinately fond. The whole atmosphere was one of preparation for a battle or a siege. Ren could not help thinking that if the *Imaiz'* influence should ever bring to pass a revolution, Castle Di Guaard would probably be the last place to fall to the insurgents.

That Di Guaard was mad was no news to Ren, but having come from more civilized worlds he had forgotten that, without psychiatry and the overriding authority of the state, madness has no checks. Even more appalling was the realization that the gross madman whose chambers Ren now entered was undisputed lord of his own castle and held life or death control over a considerable number of soldiers and slaves. Even Sonel Taw, the castellan, went patently in fear of his terrifying master and excused himself rapidly at the chamber door.

As he crossed the floor alone Ren felt the full impact of the man. Delph Di Guaard was leaning over a huge table, his back to the door. His vast bulk suggested superhuman strength and even from the rear Ren could sense the aura of power of the man's tyrannic personality. He found himself almost afraid of the moment when the creature would turn and face him.

"Well?" Di Guaard's voice made the chamber reverberate. "What news do you bring of the Tyrene?"

"No news of the Tyrene, my Lord. I come about other matters." Ren controlled his voice with a confident, faultless presence. His verbal bouts with Magno Vestevaal had been excellent training for this occasion.

"Other matters?" Di Guaard shouted. "In time of war?" He swung about and Ren looked unflinchingly into the staring, accusing eyes of the mad lord. The fellow's visage writhed constantly with the underplay of some shaded thoughts in which anger and comprehension chased each other continuously through the flesh. "Ah, an outworlder. That would explain your naiveté. You must be Agent Ren. My castellan mumbled something about your coming. Well you've come to the right man. Have the Tyrene sacked your warehouse, slaughtered your servants or raped your daughters?" His mouth almost drooled at the vision.

"None of those," said Ren. "My news is more serious. It concerns the very existence of Anharitte itself."

Di Guaard hit the table a heavy blow with his hand. "I knew it! I told that fool Di Irons that one day the pirates would attack in force. You see here—" His thick fingers jabbed pointlessly at a torn chart on the table. "That's the reason why so many of their ships have congregated to the north. We have constant sightings of a hundred, two hundred ships—they say an armada. And I, Di Guaard, am the only one in the three hills who keeps his defenses ready. The rest of them think me mad, but now it's I who am proven sane. Don't you agree that unpreparedness in time of war is mad?"

"Of course," said Ren, determined to remain undaunted. "But the danger I speak of comes from within Anharitte, not from the sea."

Di Guaard's scowl changed to an expression of intense consternation. "You mean the Tyrene came overland across T'Empte?" He consulted his charts again and then threw them furiously back on the table. He rounded on Ren in a frightening blaze of anger.

"Liar! What mischief are you selling, merchant? Dion-daizan keeps close watch on the inland waters. If any Tyrene were coming that way he'd have been sure to let me know."

"Listen to me." Ren let his voice grow loud for the first time. "While you watch for the Tyrene an even greater threat is growing right beneath your feet. Dion-dazian is educating slaves. If enough become educated there will be a revolution that will ruin us all more surely than any pirate raid."

"Really?" Di Guaard's face lit up with the malicious interest of a wolf about to tear apart a particularly succulent lamb. "And what makes an outworld merchant's lackey presume to tell the lords of Anharitte what they should or should not do with their slaves? Dion's more capable than most at controlling an uprising among his bondslaves. Dion's more than capable of controlling anything." As he said this last phrase, Di Guaard's voice fell to an unexpected wistfulness, as if even he acknowledged the power of the Imaiz.

"I didn't say he wasn't," said Ren, suddenly forced on to the defensive. "My point was that his activities are likely to cause an uprising."

The suggestion was wasted on Di Guaard, who was rounding the table with a maniacal expression of glee on his face. His gross hands were shaping themselves to fit Ren's throat.

"Shall I tell you, merchant, the real purpose of your visit? You're an agent of the Tyrene trying to cause dissension and to divert my attention. You want to get your ships up the Aprillo while I turn my back to watch Thirdhill for the rising of a few slaves. Well, you've not succeeded. I've been watching your wily tricks too long. I know you— and I know you're out there waiting for the chance to strike. Do you take me for a fool?"

Ren retreated uneasily before the big man's advance. He was not sure but the fellow's derangement might extend to his doing actual physical damage. And Ren did not dare to draw his blaster—circumstances might force him to use it. He could kill Di Guaard in self-defense, but the

political repercussions would certainly end the
Company's tenure on Roget. He continued his
protests while the madman stalked him with a
grim and ferocious amusement.

Finally he realized that flight was the only sen-
sible expedient. Gauging his distance carefully,
he ran for the door and slammed it behind him.
Something heavy and ceramic shattered to pieces
against the wood inside the room. From the insane laughter that followed he deduced that Di
Guaard was unlikely to continue in pursuit, but
for Ren the incident was a humiliating failure. He
was not going to gain from Di Guaard the support
he needed.

In an alcove at the head of the stair Ren found
Sonel Taw ostensibly waiting to escort him out of
the establishment. Ren thought it more than probable that Taw had been listening at Di Guaard's
door and had been surprised by the sudden
emergence of the visitor. Since the castellan
would probably be called upon to account for why
he had allowed a Tyrene spy to enter his master's
presence, Ren did not blame the man for seeking
information in order to prepare his lies in advance. The life of a castellan in the service of Di
Guaard could certainly be no sinecure.

This conjecture, however, was not an idle
thought. If Sonel Taw took the trouble to keep
himself fully informed of everything that took
place in the castle he could probably be of more
use to the company's cause than Di Guaard himself. Ren decided to test the truth of this proposition. When they were safely out of the keep and
crossing the inner bailey he turned to Taw mean-
ingfully.

"The Lord Di Guaard is plentifully supplied with information regarding the whereabouts and movements of pirates. I find this odd, since common consent has it that the pirates are no more."

The castellan looked past him carefully.

"It could be," he said, "that common consent is wrong, Agent Ren. Di Guaard has many spies. They report frequently and are rewarded with coin. It has been suggested that many of the things they tell are more than the truth, since they are well paid for what they say. But there's another who tells much and yet asks nothing in return."

"Specifically who?" asked Ren.

"Your friend the *Imaiz*." Taw was craftily watching the agent out of the corners of his eyes. "He claims to keep watch over the inland waters and brings special reports regularly to Lord Di Guaard. Di Guaard is always much pleased to see him, and the wizard quiets his tantrums considerably. With so much impressive support for the existence of pirates, do you think it wise for you or me to disbelieve?"

The castellan was purposely mocking his own words, hinting at the existence of a conspiracy—a development Ren had already deduced for himself. If Di Guaard was mad enough to believe that the Tyrene plunderers still functioned, others could gainfully manufacture evidence in support of that belief. For some the incentive was obvious—a purse full of money. For others, such as Sonel Taw and members of the castle household, support of the myth probably meant the continuance of their livelihood and possibly their lives. But what had Dion-daizan to gain from the charade?

"Do you know why I came to see Di Guaard today?"

Sonel Taw shrugged. His wizened old face wrinkled with guile. "Anharitte is full of the news that you and the Imaiz have joined in feud. It's reasonable to assume that you came here looking for an ally."

"A fair assumption." Ren looked at him searchingly. "But I didn't find one. At least not in Delph Di Guaard. But now I ask myself about you."

"To help you in a feud against the Imaiz?" Sonel Taw was obviously worried by the suggestion.

"Not actively, of course," Ren reassured him. "But I need information about Dion-daizan. I need to know why he humors Di Guaard and what he might gain from such a curious association. I'd like to be informed of when he visits Castle Di Guaard—at what hour he's likely to return from such visits and what routes he'll most probably use. In short, I need to know anything about Dion-daizan that might conceivably be turned to his disadvantage. And if your ear is as well affixed to locks as it appears to be, you'll already know that the Company has an excellent history of rewarding its friends for their time and vigilance."

"I've often heard as much," said Sonel Taw. "And that's the type of friendship a man could learn to appreciate. But if someone made this information available to you—would it be certain that no news of it ever got back to Di Guaard?"

"All information is treated in the strictest confidence. Nothing can ever be traced back to its source through me. Nor do I keep records of what moneys have been paid. Or to whom."

"Then I think you may have gained another friend," said Taw. "Not that I would hold any man of Di Guaard's household capable of subversion—but should a messenger be received claiming to have been sent by me, it would seem reasonable that he might be believed. And if a friend might bless my savings so that they multiply, I should not, through humility, be offended."

"I'll bear that in mind," Ren said. "I'm a believer in humility's achieving its just rewards. You know, talking with you has been an education. I'm sure my knowledge of events in Castle Di Guaard will improve."

They had passed from the inner bailey to the outer during this conversation and were now entering one of the two formidable gatehouses that gave access to the town. Upon Sonel Taw's approach the guard sprang meticulously into action. Taw had merely to wave his hand to initiate the raising of the portcullis. In the roof of the gate tunnel were slits through which all kinds of merciless fire and bolts could be discharged. Beyond it, the gate of heavy wood plated with iron lay between the overseeing flanking-towers. Farther still the outward path was confronted by the outworks of a barbican tower.

Ren made a mental note that nobody could enter or leave without Sonel Taw's permission and the cooperation of the guards. By a mental inversion he decided that the walls and gates, being impregnable to all save modern technological assault, not only formed a rare defense position—but would also make a very secure prison. He had no immediate use for this information, but he stored it in his mind for future reference. There were some advantages in being an outworlder—it gave him a unique perspective on installations traditionally designed for specific local purposes. Ren felt that his tenure in Anharitte, as elsewhere, was bound to generate some new values and he was determined to be the first not only to recognize but also to apply these altered truths to the Company's and his own advantage.

X

As he walked past the wayward, half-timbered houses of the quaint alleys and streets, Ren's speculations were soon eclipsed by a more immediate concern. His recent conversation with Alek Hardun had shaken him severely. Hardun had been introduced as a professional trouble shooter. Ren now felt that Hardun's real function was that of a professional trouble-maker. The equipment in the space-going laboratory that was the battle cruiser was directed primarily to one end—the sophisticated extermination of people.

For all his merchant-acumen and ambition, Ren still had reservations about the deliberate taking of life. His worldliness had inured him to the fact that some extremes of provocation could only be resolved by bloodshed. In self-defense or fair fighting, losers were apt to have to pay the irrevocable penalty. This was a fact of life and Ren accepted it, but Hardun's projected subtle poisoning of dozens—if not hundreds—of people who would be mainly unaware that they were the subjects of an attack stuck in Ren's throat. This he regarded as an atrocity, a treatment suitable for the extermination of lice and vermin but not to be confused with the humane waging of a battle.

Alek Hardun had chided Ren for expressing these sentiments.

"You're confusing the issues, Tito," he had said. "You were born several centuries too late. We know the ancients used to impose rules on warfare, presumably to prolong the enjoyment of the game. But the brutal fact is that we're here to fight—we're here to win. I've offered you a dozen virtually foolproof ways of winning and you've rejected them all because of some romantic notion that the enemy deserves a chance.

"Do you think the bowmen stood a chance when the cannon was invented? Do you think the artillery stood a chance against the introduction of nuclear weapons? Within the whole spectrum of devices for furthering man's inhumanity to man, you have the temerity to stop at some arbitrary point and say: 'Death devices on the left are sporting and humane while those on the right aren't.' Such a stand is neither logical nor intelligent. And if you can't bring yourself to do the job you've started to do, I'm damned if I won't finish it for you."

There had been more, a lot more. Ren had become increasingly angry and Hardun had become more professionally cruel and taunting. He had effectively dismantled Ren's plans to conduct a campaign against the Imaiz and had produced alternative suggestions which Ren could only regard with horror. The effect of that conversation had lingered a long time in Ren's mind and he was determined to compare the strength of his convictions with those of the director. Vestevaal, unfortunately, had been away for several days, making a tour of Company trading installations, and Ren had been left with the question festering in his mind.

When Ren reached his office chambers the director still had not returned. Ren found instead that his computer printout terminal had been busy. In it lay the precious list of slaves carefully culled from reconstructed histories to show those who could most possibly be agents of the Imaiz. He scanned the list anxiously, but the names meant nothing to him. For Catuul Gras, who knew everyone and everything in Anharitte, the situation would be different. Ren stuffed the list into his pocket and hastened to the Lodge of the Society of Pointed Tails.

As usual, the senior scribe was expecting him. Ren speculated that there must be very few movements of importance of which the Pointed Tails were unaware, such was the superlative nature of their spy web in Anharitte. He laid the list before Catuul, who examined it carefully. For some unstated reason his enthusiasm was not apparent.

"I'll have our slave masters investigate this without delay—but discreetly. No word of it must get out until we're sure. If the suspects became suspicious it would be easy for them to desert back to Magda."

"I'll leave it to you," said Ren. "But it's still action only in a negative sense. It's a defensive move. What I must have from you is some scheme with a positive effect."

"And you'll have it, friend Tito. I promised you a scheme of feud and harassment against Diondaizan and this has now been prepared. To your outworld eyes it may seem a little superficial—but believe me, in terms of effectiveness in

Anharitte its cumulative value is equivalent to a
major disaster."

"I'll accept that you know what you're doing.
But time's becoming critical, Catuul. I'm under
pressure to destroy the influence of the Imaiz and
to do it fast. If your scheme can't produce results
quickly we'll be forced into taking a more direct
line and attacking Dion-daizan himself."

"What sort of time-scale did you have in
mind?"

"I think a couple of weeks only. Hardun is already campaigning with the Free Trade Council
for permission to take a tougher line. I think I can
stall them for a while, but we mustn't miss any
opportunity to hit Dion hard."

"You're worried about something, aren't you,
friend Tito?" The scribe was suddenly questioning.

"Yes, I am. I've come to have a great deal of
respect for your culture, Catuul. As a Company
man I can't afford to risk losing access to the
spaceport, but outside of that proviso I believe
you've a right to settle your problems in your own
way and without your society's becoming unduly
contaminated by outworld interference. But I'm
afraid that if you don't settle the Imaiz soon, a
more ruthless faction among the Free Traders will
bring such pressures to bear that Anharitte will
never be the same place after."

"I'm aware of the situation," said Catuul
gravely. "I've seen what the coming of the
spaceport has done to us unwittingly. Thus I've
no doubt of what would be the outcome of more
deliberate manipulation. Frankly, that's why we
opted to work with you. You've an appreciation of

what a separate identity means both to an individual and to a culture. That's something rare in
an outworlder."

"You can thank the director. I guess I caught my
attitude from him."

"Well, here's our proposal. Dion-daizan main-
tains many large estates and farms in Magda province. The value of the produce is a major source of
Magda's income."

"More than the spaceport revenue?" Ren was
learning something new.

"Certainly much more. But the point I wish to
make is that the Imaiz' success in his estate policy
depends on close coordination of the various estates and markets. If we destroy that coordination,
his growing and marketing schemes will fall
apart. Prices will rise, setting popular sympathy
against him—and he will soon acquire huge
stocks of surplus. He will also find himself with
excess manpower and will be forced to start selling slaves on a massive scale. A disaster of such
consequence will smash his myth of omnipotence
as nothing else will."

"How could you bring this about?" asked Ren.

"Dion operates a schedule of runners who daily
travel between the various marketing centers and
estates. We could stop a high proportion of these
runners getting through—and in some cases substitute false messages of our own."

Ren was enthusiastic. "When an organization
as large and as dispersed as that hits communications trouble, things can come widly unstuck.
How long would it take to show real effect?"

"Many weeks, I'm afraid. But the main harvests
are nearly due. If Dion were left with those on his

hands, he'd be in real trouble both with his estates and with the populations he normally supplies. Of course, he'll send out armed patrols to try and prevent our interference—but the clansmen were born to the game and Dion doesn't have anything like the army he'd need to stop us."

"So all you really require to bring the *Imaiz* to his knees is sufficient time?"

"Time and money. I want to bring in some of the provincial societies, because the area to be covered is immense. Though we shall start hurting the *Imaiz* immediately, the effect won't be apparent in the markets for some weeks. Therefore you've got to hold off the Free Traders while we do it our way."

"I don't have that much influence myself, but I'll try to make the director see the sense of it. In the meantime, muster your forces and make a start. If we can get a good scheme under way we'll have a sure method of resisting those who want to do it the rough way."

Vestevaal, on his return, gravely heard out Ren's problems.

"I wasn't aware that Hardun was here in any capacity other than a technical backup for you. I know he has an allegiance to Rance, but this is our fight. You've every right to complain if he's contemplating any actions other than those specifically agreed to by you. I respect your judgment on this issue, Tito, and I'm damned if I'm going to see you pressured into making a mistake."

"I've seen his copy of the Free Trade security subcommittee directive giving him power to act on Roget. And that battle cruiser of his is a fully equipped civil murder weapon. So I want a plain answer, Director—am I in charge here or has Hardun the right of unilateral action? Because I want no part of some of the ideas he's outlined to me."

"You say you've seen his directive? Can you recall who signed it?"

"Po Cresado, as I remember."

"Damn! I thought as much. The merchant-world pressure lobby. You can take it from me, Tito, that his directive doesn't have the consent of the full council. Unfortunately the merchant worlds do predominate on the security subcommittee. It looks as though the internal political battles of the council have become extended to include affairs on Roget."

"Are you going to let them get away with it?"

"Of course not. But it'll take a full council session to settle the issue. I'm afraid I'll have to return there to get the matter straight. Do you think you can contain things until I get back?"

"I'll try, but I've no jurisdiction over Hardun in the face of that directive. And if he thinks you're out to stop him, he's likely to move fast."

"Then try pretending to work with him for a while. It might just be that he'll actually do the job for you—and at a fraction of the price. Though I fear that even our friend Alek may not find the project as easy as he thinks."

"Can you explain that to me?"

"I mean the *Imaiz* himself is under no doubts about Hardun or his infernal space machine."

"How could you possibly know that?"

"My dear Ren, what do you think Zinder and I talked about while we were waiting to register her bond? She gave me Dion's ultimatum—either I remove Hardun and the battle cruiser or Dion-daizan will do the job himself. Until now I've had reservations. But from what you've just told me I can see the justification. I'll set out to have Hardun and his ship removed—but don't feel surprised if somebody does the job for me."

"I've told Catuul to go ahead with his plan to cause disruption of Dion-daizan's estate-management policies. That will at least give me a lever I can use to slow Hardun down. But it will be difficult to stop him if he does want to try a decisive stroke of his own."

"Then play it carefully, Tito. Take advantage of his successes and don't become implicated in his failures. That way you can stay on top and the name of the Company stays clean."

"You've just expressed a philosophy," said Ren, "that makes me appreciate why you have so much influence in the Free Trade Council. You never lose, do you?"

"I can't afford to lose," said Magno Vestevaal seriously. "And believe me, I've a few tricks up my sleeve the rest of the council haven't even thought of yet. If all goes well at the council meeting, I'll probably go on to Terra before returning here. I've been developing a few thoughts of my own about how to deal with the *Imaiz*—and if I can get acceptance of my ideas on Terra I can assure you that Alek Hardun won't be rated as any serious sort of competition."

XI

Following through on the next part of his campaign to seek influence with the Anharitte nobility, Ren had dispatched a message to Krist Di Rode requesting an audience the following morning. The reply was favorable. Before he retired, however, Ren took advantage of the caution offered by Di Irons—he posted a guard in his chambers lest the *Imaiz* should feel inclined to take the initiative. An attempted assassination did not seem likely, but Ren had been an agent long enough to learn that warnings from an indigenous source were better not disregarded. Fortunately the night passed without incident and, at the appointed hour the next day, Ren traveled to the most eastern point of Firsthill and presented himself at Castle Di Rode.

The contrasts between this establishment and that of Di Guaard made him realize what a fortune Di Guaard must spend on useless defense projects. Di Rode was a prodigious spender, but his considerable income from spaceport revenues had not been wasted. Castle Di Rode was bathed in an atmosphere of opulence and splendor.

Though the castle was slightly smaller than that of Di Guaard, it differed in none of its essential features except that the walls and mural towers of Di Rode displayed none of the former's austerity

of outline. Here the masonry was fully overgrown
with a magnificent wealth of copper-burnished
creeping vines, which garnished the old stone
like an overlay of finely wrought metal. Expenditure on the guard was nominal, and mainly slaves
and serving-men in splendid costumes tended to
gatehouses and the trim gardens.

Everywhere Ren sensed the hand of a connois-
seur of gracious living, not the least extravagance
being the maintenance of the gardens and the
beautiful decoration of the halls. Di Rode was
obviously an intellectual and an artist, possessed
of an unerring sense of the overall unity of his
establishment as an aesthetic whole. The numerous slaves were well tended and nourished
and probably chosen for their clean, straight
limbs and physical fitness. In the whole castle he
discerned not one slave whose back bore the
telltale scars of whip or wire. The whole atmosphere was one of serenity and quietude. This,
thought Ren, was the way money was intended to
be spent.

The keep of Castle Di Rode was built into the
southeast extremity of the inner bailey. It held a
commanding view over the Aprillo river and
across the shipping lanes that connected with the
inland waterways. The keep itself was no longer a
simple structure. Later buildings along the walls
of the inner bailey had crept around the base of the
round-tower and risen to a height equal to the
walls themselves. Thus the entrance to the keep
was no longer gained by crossing a sterile courtyard, but rather through a delightfully random
series of halls, libraries, galleries, corridors and
sweeping staircases.

As Ren followed his young slavecaste guide he found himself, unaccountably at first, becoming increasingly discomforted. This feeling was in part associated with the increasing richness of the perfumes and incense with which the air was saturated, but this was only a factor and not the prime cause of his unease. A gradual analysis of his feelings made him conscious of the fact that the rooms through which he passed were in a careful sequence of ascending extravagance and descending taste, and had already attained a level where the lavish dissipation of resources made nonsense both of the function and the intrinsic value of the items involved. This was so extreme a contrast with the exterior of the castle and the earlier rooms, that the only answer that suggested itself to Ren was that Di Rode, like Delph Di Guaard, was beset by advancing madness.

Ren's senses protested the wrongness they recorded. When he reached the confines of the keep itself his feelings heightened to revulsion despite his efforts to contain them. Here was monumental waste with neither art nor comfort to commend it. Even the occasional alcoves were lit by candelabra mounted on the heads and shoulders of undraped slaves who stood with statuesque patience, performing a function no more important than could have been achieved by an iron pin driven into the wall.

This final debasement of living humanity caused Ren as acute a pain as he had experienced on seeing the degraded labor force at Castle Di Guaard. Profitable exploitation of others was a human weakness Ren could comprehend. To

waste members of the species by forcing them to
fill functions usually performed by inanimate objects was, in his view, irrational and completely
indefensible. Fortunately he regained both his
outward composure and his objectivity before he
turned the final corner to come face-to-face with
Krist Di Rode himself.

He needed all his resources to contain his
amazement. He had been shown into a bare cell,
whose stone walls were as stark and undressed as
had been the human candelabra he had passed. A
high, square window without glazing looked out
only to the blankness of an empty sky, and the
shaped wooden bench on which the Lord Di Rode
reclined offered no possible aspect of comfort.
The floor of stone flags was unrelieved by carpet
and the ceilings of arched stone had neither light
nor beauty.

Di Rode himself was also a shock to Ren. He had
imagined an older, more sophisticated type of
man, perhaps one trying to ward off old age by the
frantic pursuit of new experience. Instead, he was
confronted by a pallid figure of a man in his early
thirties, with a face which epitomized dissipation
and overindulgence yet still possessed an un-
deniable strength. Ren had the feeling that this
curious lord had tried and become dissatisfied
with almost every aesthetic and sensual experience known to man. The physical dissolution was
manifest, but the evidence was that the intellectual and aesthetic interest was yet unquenched.
While Di Rode's face held a searching interest and
unquestionable intelligence, it was obvious that
unrestricted wealth, like absolute power, had
wrought a remarkable corrosion on its owner.

With a trader's acumen Ren had summarized this much of the man before he began to speak, subtly modifying his arguments in order to stress aspects of Dion-daizan's activities that might have an effect on Di Rode. The latter listened to him attentively, stopping him occasionally to query some chain of fact that led to Ren's conclusions. Then he remained for a long period in contemplative thought.

"To summarize, Agent Ren, you've presented an excellent case predicting what Dion's policy might take away from me. But you've mentioned nothing about the loss of what I receive from Dion while I remain his friend."

"We have access to the resources of all the known universe," said Ren. "There's nothing that Dion can supply that we can't better. Nothing at all."

"Does that include understanding?" Di Rode was quietly mocking. "Do you have access to some cosmic source of that?"

The unexpectedness of the question fazed Ren momentarily. "I don't follow you."

"Think about it. If you had an unrestricted opportunity to indulge whatever whims you chose—how long would it take you to destroy yourself?"

"I don't know," admitted Ren. "I'd at least have one hell of a fine time finding out."

"Spoken with all the complacency of one who'll never have the opportunity! But what does a man need when he's tasted everything, satiated every appetite and yielded to every conceivable temptation?"

Ren did not answer. The question was beyond

the scope of his imagination.

Di Rode continued. "He needs understanding. He needs discipline. He needs a father-figure who can pick up the mess he's become, squeeze out the rot and put back enough self-respect for the man to become a man again. That's what Dion supplies to me—psychological rehabilitation. He picks up the pieces when I've torn myself apart and establishes new values to replace those I've lost. Do you have something better to offer as a replacement for Dion's prowess with people?"

"We have doctors—"

"Doctors are for the sick," said Di Rode cuttingly. "I'm not sick—just unusually privileged. With Dion's aid I can probably crowd the pleasures of a hundred lifetimes into one. So you see, Ren, there's nothing you can offer me in exchange for my allegiance. Wizards don't come in tonnage lots."

Ren was about to make a reply when Di Rode got up from the bench and made as though to call a servant. The agent's gaze did not follow the hedonistic lord, but remained fixed in fascination on the bench from which Di Rode had risen. He saw now for the first time that the entire surface was covered with upward-pointing metal spines, like a bed of nails. In an agony of realization his eyes traveled involuntarily to Di Rode's back.

Krist Di Rode was watching his perplexity with some amusement. With a swift movement he dropped the single drape that covered his back and allowed Ren to examine his flesh. There were slight indentations from the pressure of the barbs, but otherwise the skin was undamaged. In contrast, however, the open weave of the drape had been severely cut. Ren looked again to the sharp spines of the couch and again back to Di Rode. By any normal reasoning, Di Rode's back should have been lacerated to an extremely serious extent. Instead, the young lord was laughing and the main discomfort was Ren's.

"Well, Agent Ren—do you still think you can do better than Dion-daizan?"

Ren shook his head, not trusting himself to speak. He suspected, not for the first time, that he was fighting a battle quite impossible for him to win. With Dion's influence removed, Delph Di Guaard would go beserk and Krist Di Rode would destroy himself. With such powerful nobility removed, the social structure of the three hills, undermined as it was, would slowly begin to disintegrate as surely as if the Imaiz were still pushing it. Dion-daizan had raised a social conscience and all the old forces of tradition would be hard-pressed to put that evolving creature back to bed.

As Ren came to the square of the fruit market he could see Catuul Gras waiting for him on the steps of his office chambers. He hastened over and the scribe followed him to safety behind closed doors before he would reveal the nature of his concern.

"Something's gone wrong." Catuul's face was grave. "The list of slaves you gave us—it was incorrect."

"What do you mean?"

"We took the slaves whose names were on the list. It didn't seem right, because most of them were well trusted and known to us. But even under pressure they gave us absolutely nothing. Most of them claimed never to have been with the Imaiz."

"Surely that's no more than you'd have expected them to say?"

"True. But on further examination we found their statements to be correct. Dr. Hardun has given us a list of our own sympathizers—and none of Dion's men at all."

"Ridiculous!"

"It's all here." Catuul Gras laid a sheaf of papers on the table. "Check for yourself. No man on that list has ever spent more than thirty-six hours in Magda and most of them haven't been there at all."

Scowling, Ren reached for the microwave communicator and called the spaceport. Alek Hardun was a long time answering.

"Tito? What's eating you?"

"What in hell are you trying to do, Alek? That list of slaves you sent was the diametric opposite of what it was supposed to represent."

"Now don't run off the spool, Tito! You asked me to reconstruct histories for a selected group of salves and to notify you of those who'd served bond with the *Imaiz* for a year or longer. That's exactly what I've done."

"Correction. That's exactly what you've not done. Catuul tells me no slave on that list has spent longer than two days in Magda."

"Hold it! That wasn't an automatic computer printout you received. We verified that list before it went on transmission. There's no possibility of an error in the data we sent you."

"Yet I'm assured the list is one hundred per cent wrong. What the hell's going on?"

"Let's check first that you have the right list. Watch your computer terminal and I'll give it to you again."

Ren watched as the computer printout began to spit forth names. When it had finished, he compared it with the papers Catuul had given to him. "How's that?" asked Hardun.

"It agrees with the first set exactly. There's not an error in the pack."

"Yet you insist they're not the names you want?"

"The names you've given me are also on the select list of Pointed Tails' least probable suspects."

"I see!" Hardun was serious. "How many names appear on your list, Tito?"

"Seventeen. You should know—you've transmitted it."

"Not on your life. My list contained seventeen names, but I transmitted only sixteen of them."

"What?"

"I said sixteen, Tito. All of whom I can guarantee have been at Magda for at least three years and most much longer. If you've just received a list of seventeen names, there's only one conclusion— the list you're receiving is not the one I'm transmitting. Somebody else has access to your terminal line. They're intercepting what I'm sending and substituting a list of their own."

"Damn!" Ren considered the enormity of the prospect. Most of the Company's business transactions were reported via his terminal to the spaceport computers for processing and onward transmission via the FTL radio links. The director's reports on the state of the feud with Diondaizan went out over the same channel. The thought of unauthorized access to the terminal linkage made his blood run cold. With a chill creeping up his spine, he turned the instrument off.

"Can you spare me some linesmen, Alek? My terminal is on a wired circuit with the spaceport. I can only assume it's been tapped."

"Not only tapped," said Hardun. "I'd suspect that it's being consistently monitored by an on-line computing complex compatible with that at the spaceport. The insertion of a substitute list at that juncture is no mean feat of technology. What the hell have they got up there at Magda?"

"I wish I knew. All the signs now are that they've a modern technological workshop that can match anything we can produce. This has to put a new face on how we approach the attack on the Imaiz—but I'll take the matter up with you personally. I don't even trust this microwave voice link now."

"That's wise," said Hardun. "But before I sign off I'll read you the list of names you should have received."

He did so. Ren copied them faithfully and handed the results to Catuul Gras. The scribe compared them with another list and shook his head concernedly.

"The names you've given me match the list of slaves who've escaped in the last two days. We presume they've gone to Magda, though the evidence isn't clear. It would seem the devil has recalled his own."

Finding the actual position of the line tap was difficult. Because Anharitte had no telephone and no electric services, the customary array of available poles was absent from the landscape. When

Ren had decided to bring his office into the fruit market in Anharitte proper, he had found it necessary to arrange for his wire link with the spaceport to be laid across private land wherever he could purchase the goodwill. The line now took a circuitous route across roofs, under eaves, around gables and dormer windows, and generally progressed in a most unorthodox manner until it ran free of the town and came to the western slopes of Firsthill. From there it ran across the country on Company-owned poles parallel to the Provincial Route that skirted the spaceport.

Despite the apparent opportunity for interference with the line in the town itself it was, curiously enough, on one of the poles on the open stretch of road that the tap was eventually found. The line had been split and both ends coupled into a neat black cable that ran unobtrusively down the pole and disappeared deep into the sandy soil of the provincial plain. Attempts to trace the path of the unauthorized cable proved tiresome and expensive and they were finally abandoned. Its general direction was, as Ren had known it would be, toward Magda. The depth and security of its lodgment showed it to have been buried at about the same time as Ren's own cable had been installed.

This latter fact alone made the agent squirm. A great volume of confidential Company business had been fed into the line over the past few years. Had the *Imaiz* been operating for a trade competitor, the Company could have suffered extreme losses as the result of this unanticipated leakage of information. There was no evidence that the knowledge the *Imaiz* must have gained had been used to the Company's disadvantage—but it was a late time to realize that one's commercial future lay in the hands of a sworn enemy.

Nor was Ren's temper improved by a further consideration.

From his terminal, by means of signature codes, he had access not only to Company computer data banks at the spaceport, but also to the spaceport's common computer banks. With the right sort of intercept equipment the Imaiz, too, would have had similar access to the same data banks and, by extrapolation there would scarcely seem to have been a commercial transaction on Roget of which the master of Magda need have remained unaware.

As a commercial blunder the situation was without parallel. The only mitigating factor for those involved was that no one could reasonably have suspected that on a relatively undeveloped planet like Roget there existed either the equipment or the technology to make this sophisticated form of espionage a fact. The strength of Diondaizan lay as much in what he concealed as in what he revealed. Wryly Ren wondered how many other surprises the Imaiz still had up his sleeve.

XII

Despite his growing antipathy for Alek Hardun, Ren was now forced to visit the spaceport in order to continue the Company's business transactions. This was because he suspected he could trust the security of neither the wire circuit nor the microwave link. Although he tried to stay out of Hardun's way, it was inevitable that the latter would learn of his coming and seek him out.

"You wouldn't be trying to avoid me, would you, Tito?"

"Why should I?" Ren's answer was couched in a frame of aggrieved innocence. "I've been very busy, that's all."

"I just wondered." Hardun was probing. "I mean, we've not yet completed our little chat on ways of removing the *Imaiz*. And they tell me Director Vestevaal has made a hurried trip back to Free Trade Central. I naturally wondered what was brewing."

"I wouldn't know. The director mentioned something to me about visiting Terra, but I'm not exactly in his confidence."

This was so patent a lie that Hardun did not even pretend to believe it.

"Very well, Tito! If you want to play it close to the chest that's your affair. Rance Intelligence will give me all the answers I need, so don't let the director think he's acting too cleverly."

"I don't see how you'd know," Ren said critically. "You're scarcely in his class."

For a moment a spear of anger burned in Hardun's eyes. Then, with amazing composure, he turned the expression of malice aside and overlaid it with a veneer of genial charm.

"Look, Tito—I know we have our differences on the way the job's to be done, but we're still here for a common purpose. We mustn't forget the Imaiz is a very clever enemy. Nothing could suit him better than to have us divided. Let's not play into his hands. How's your campaign going?"

"Slowly, but I think we've got it made. The Pointed Tails have produced a scheme for disrupting Dion's holdings right through Magda Province. I've been into it in detail and I don't see how they can fail. Given nine months we'll have the Imaiz begging for alms in the streets."

"Nine months!" The veneer of geniality was stretched taut. "And Vestevaal settled for that? It shouldn't take nine days to settle a little issue like this. Somebody's going soft."

"That's your view, Alek. But you haven't studied the local conditions as I have. Believe me, we have to play this one very softly."

"I accept that it's your fight, Tito, but I'd like to make one strike just to prove to you that I can do as I say."

"Then make it, Alek. I don't seem to be able to stop you," said Ren unexpectedly. "But I'm not supporting you and I don't wish to be implicated in any way. Furthermore, if you make a hash of it and the whole thing blows up into an interplanetary row, I'll set up such a howl for your skin that even Rance'll have to throw you to the wolves. As far as I'm concerned you're a Rance combat unit and nothing to do with legitimate Free Trade at all."

"I can see you've been doing your homework." Hardun's acknowledgment was a grudging acceptance of the terms. "I'll make the strike tonight and guarantee you undisputed access to Castle Magda in the morning. I'll even have a squad of Rance commandos standing by to do any mopping up that may be required. It's about time you tradesmen learned that jobs like this were better left to professionals."

Under cover of the early darkness Hardun moved his murder contingent out to the plain. Because the whole episode was highly illegal in terms of Roget law, absolute secrecy was essential. For this reason the most opportune site, that between the Via Arens and the Space Canal, could not be used, for fear of chance observation. The alternative site was the rising banks of the wilder country almost centrally between the Provincial Route and the Old Coast Road. Here there was almost no chance of observation during the hours of darkness, though by day it would have lain under the scrutiny of the watchtowers and the great keep of Castle Di Guaard. The rocket's trajectory thus lay slightly over the northwest corner of Firsthill, but such was the precision of the apparatus that the chance of premature fallout on the town was negligible.

All day had been spent by Hardun's technicians in calculating the course coordinates and carefully calibrating the equipment to guarantee the pinpoint accuracy necessary to ensure that the deadly black canister was delivered precisely inside the confines of the castle and not dispersed across Thirdhill and its township. The position of the central point of the castle had been determined with micrometers by laser triangulation. A radar lock from the battle cruiser and a second one from a manpack station on the northern slopes of Secondhill gave the necessary references for faultless radio guidance of the missile from its mobile launcher to the castle. All this preparation had been leisurely and time-consuming. Speed was not important, but it was absolutely vital that the payload of sinister cargo fell cleanly inside the castle walls.

The toxin had come from a stockpile of horrifying weapons on Rance. Its rate of diffusion under all conditions of still and moving air were known with great precision. The metering and dispersion could be controlled to a nicety to permit an almost exact spread of effect before destructive oxidation by the atmosphere rendered it not only harmless but virtually undetectable. In a situation such as its release inside an isolated citadel like Magda, the great walls themselves would serve somewhat to contain the dispersion, so that little, if any, chance existed of its affecting anyone outside the castle walls. Inside the walls its potential was conservatively estimated at seven thousand per cent overkill. By morning the best bacteriologists in the universe, while they might have their suspicions, would find it impossible to produce proof of the deliberate nature of the hit-and-run plague whose one and only symptom was immediate death. The dispersion warhead was self-destroying and would leave no incriminating remains.

Ren himself had no stomach at all for the project. Fortunately he had retained his resolve and refused to take any part in the venture. To protect the company's name—in the event of any future investigation of the pending atrocity—he had felt it necessary that he should establish an indestructible alibi by being seen in Anharitte at the time the act was committed. He therefore left the spaceport in advance of the murder party and traveled the Via Arena to pick up a crew of stave-bearers for his cushion-craft slightly before dusk.

The garish ligroin flares of the trading stalls around the arena were well in evidence as he passed. Ren stopped and made a few purchases in order to establish his location at that time. The streets, as usual at that hour, were crowded with an aimless, nonchalant throng, none of whom seemed to appreciate any need for a clear and unobstructed highway. Mule carts, loaded to ridiculous heights with straw baskets, seemed eternally to be in his way and it took Ren nearly an hour to negotiate the cushion-craft the two kilometers from the Black Rock to the foot of the Trade Road. Ren bore this ordeal with fortitude, not daring to express his anxiety or his crying need to be in a location where more people would recognize him and be able to vouch for his presence on that particular evening. Fortunately the Trade Road was clearer and the craft was poled easily up the slopes and out to the broad brow of Firsthill.

It was here that he first heard the explosions. In reactive shock he at first thought that the rocket must have misfired on its launcher. A second burst of noise, however, caused him to notice that the origin of the sounds was too far to the left to be coming from the provincial plains and was more probably coming from the guns of Di Guaard. Remembering the formidable chain-throwing cannon that Di Guaard maintained to cover the Aprillo Delta against the mythical Tyrene, Ren was able to make a guess that Hardun was in trouble. The vicious cannon atop the castle keep were being rapidly deployed against something to the west—a fact he was able to confirm when his position enabled him to see the flashes of the guns themselves. It did not take much further conjecture to appreciate that the only target to be found on the plains at this hour was Hardun and his rocket projector and the deadly rocket with which he intended to wipe out the human—not to mention humane—population of Castle Magda.

Ren reached his office chambers in a state of agonized indecision and suffering from an embarrassing lack of information. He was tempted to try to contact Alek Hardun via the microwave link, but there were dangers that some record of the conversation could implicate both himself and the Company. On the face of it, the chances of the mad Delph Di Guaard's guns being able to seek out a target on the dark plain appeared negligible. However, the hand of the Imaiz in Castle Di Guaard—and the awful coincidence of the rocket launcher on the plains under the speaking guns—threw up possibilities too haunting to be ignored.

Having parked the cushion-craft, Ren made his way to the Lodge of the Pointed Tails, where discreet information was usually available. The lodge was deserted save for a solitary guardian, who appeared to think the clan was already out on Ren's own business and was surprised that the agent had no knowledge of the fact. He, too, had no idea of why Di Guaard's guns were firing, but promised to send a runner to contact the clan and to carry news back to Ren as fast as possible. Ren returned to his office and sat waiting for the information.

It was fully an hour before Catuul Gras came to the door.

"We were looking for you earlier, Tito. Sonel Taw sent a messenger for you. When he couldn't find you, he had sense enough to come looking for me."

"I was delayed at the spaceport," said Ren. "What was the message?"

"That the *Imaiz* was expected in Castle Di Guaard tonight."

"He is?" This put a new aspect on Hardun's venture with the rocket and Ren could not conceal his surprise. This was one point on which even Alek Hardun had miscalculated.

"I laid plans for immediate ambush," said Catuul Gras, "but the *Imaiz* slipped through."

"Dion's already there, then?"

"Yes. He must have come around by the Provincial Route or the Old Coast Road. He came up Sidepath and was already in Castle Di Guaard before we got the news."

"Was anyone with him?"

"Only Zinder and Barii, I think."

"Have you any idea what Di Guaard's firing at?"

Catuul smiled. "I suspect the *Imaiz* put him up to it. It's said Dion carries strange tales about the Tyrene to Di Guaard. I'd wager the mad Delph is on top of his tower right now, firing at imaginary pirates and believing himself to be the savior of Anharitte. Still, it's better that he fires across the plains. There's no one out there to hurt. Safer than firing at the shipping on the river."

Ren felt cold and rather sick. Because of the atrocious nature of the weapon Hardun had taken out into the plain not even the Pointed Tails had been made party to the secret. The presence on Roget of such a potent outworld mass-murder instrument was not something that Ren cared to advertise—nor would the knowledge have helped his liaison with the loyal but native clan whose services he so frequently employed. His one consolation was that without radar and ranging instruments, the mad Di Guaard was unlikely actually to hit the rocket launcher. More probably, Hardun would abandon the venture and retire to the security of the spaceport. However, if Hardun continued his plan and launched the biomissile into Magda, then he would certainly fail to kill the one man on Roget who could unearth the truth behind the death of the garrison at Magda. The damage the *Imaiz* could do with that truth both on Roget and with the Galactic Federal Council could not only put an end to the free port, but could work against Free Trade right across the galaxy.

The agent became aware that the scribe was watching him curiously.

"What's on your mind, Tito?"

"Nothing," Ren lied. "But so far our feud against the *Imaiz* has been a continuing series of failures. I can't afford more. We know the *Imaiz* is in Castle Di Guaard and that some time he's going to have to come out. I don't care what it costs, Catuul, or how many other societies you need to reinforce your own men, but I want the *Imaiz* ambushed—and I want him killed. I want you to make it a point of honor that he never returns to Magda."

Catuul's intelligent eyes were probing gently, but he made no comment on his conclusions.

"As you wish, Tito. I'll make all the necessary arrangements. We'll seal Castle Di Guaard like a trap. No matter when Dion-daizan emerges there'll be good shafts and good steel waiting for him. If he ever sees Magda again, it'll be solely due to his wizardry."

Because there was nothing else he could usefully do Ren went to bed and tried to sleep. In this he was for many hours unsuccessful because he had no idea at all what pattern of news would greet him the next day. The possibilities ranged from brilliant success to tragic failure, with a range of complex permutations in between, many of which could involve him in being asked some acutely embarrassing questions. Even the certainty of failure would have allowed him to rest more easily, but he was currently immersed in a vacuum containing no answers, from which he dared not emerge to ask questions lest he betray his own foreknowledge. His surest method of defense was to profess complete ignorance of the events that took place that night.

Finally, however, he must have slept for a while. He woke again to the first gray of dawn, feeling wretched and compelled by curiosity to contact the spaceport by the microwave radio link. As he dressed and dragged himself downstairs the call alarm of his transreceiver gave a clatter that made him stop in startled shock. It was many seconds before he could bring himself to lift the handset.

"Tito?"

"Alek—what happened?"

"Happened?" Hardun's tone along foreshadowed the tale of disaster. "Di Guaard's cannon hit the launcher. The toxin dispersion canister went off prematurely and all six of the crew were dead of the plague inside five minutes. There was nothing I could do to help them."

"What about yourself?"

"I was lucky. I was following up in the radio unit truck. Di Guaard wrapped one of his chainshots around the turret and I stopped to estimate the damage. By the time I got going again the launcher was on its side and the crew was trying to run. I reversed out fast and called out the medical team from the spaceport. They got there in twenty minutes, but when they knew what toxin we had in the canister they refused to go in. It wouldn't have been much use anyway. Once that toxin's out there's no protection against it and only time and exposure can counter it."

"So we've a broken rocket launcher and six bodies out on the plain in full view of Di Guaard's watchtowers when the light gets better. Damn! Di Irons will flay us for this."

"It's still pretty misty out here. I think we're

covered until the sun comes over the hill. That gives us an hour yet to remove the mess. I've emergency tenders standing by, but we're trying to delay for as long as possible so that the toxin is fully broken down. We daren't risk losing any more men. What in the name of Jupiter possessed Di Guaard to open fire like that?"

"You don't know the hell of it," said Ren. "Even if you'd succeeded you'd still have been in trouble. The *Imaiz* wasn't at Magda. He was with Di Guaard. I suspect he was directing operations, having first explored the situation for himself. At a guess, he had all your preparations under observation—and you drove straight into a trap."

"That would figure," said Hardun sourly. "We were the victims of good espionage, perfect timing and diabolical ranging accuracy. I had the feeling that if the chain shots hadn't stopped us they would have been followed up by high explosives. As it was, the bombardment stopped shortly after the launcher got into trouble, as though they knew they had hit something vital. What are the chances of their having an infrared ranging camera at Castle Di Guaard?"

"Every chance—with the *Imaiz* behind them."

"Tito, we've got to destroy this man—and fast—or we haven't a hope of retaining Anharitte as a free port."

"I've got him bottled inside Castle Di Guaard," said Ren. "Catuul's mustering a whole army and we'll keep them in position for as long as may be required. I don't myself think Dion will attempt to come out. I think he'll sit there and wait for us to go away."

"Then this strikes me as an opportune time to

try a reconnaissance raid on Magda. I have the commandos assembled, but I'll be too busy on the plain to take the lead. Could you handle it it for me, Tito?"

"I've no great objection to a reconnaissance. And it might produce some useful information."

"Good. I'll have the men meet you at Magda Crossing in an hour's time."

"I'll be there," said Ren and went thoughtfully in search of breakfast.

XIII

There was no doubt from close quarters that Castle Magda was the most formidable of all the fortresses on the three hills. It was larger than the installation of Di Guaard, yet planned with the same paranoiac approach—the supposition that all men's hands were against it. The outer walls of massive granite blocks were probably solid for twenty meters at the base and rose sheer out of the waters of an unwelcoming moat. Even the dark streaks in the granite conspired to give the place an air of unassailable endurance.

Whoever had planned and built Magda had been a genius in his own right. There was not an inch of the wall that was not overlooked by some flanking tower, and all possible angles of approach lay under a dozen points from which a hidden defender might safely fire. It was not even possible to tell if one were being observed, so dark and numerous were the potential defense positions.

Although they were armed, the group of thirty-five Rance commandoes with Ren had strict instructions to do no more than test the defenses. They could indulge in a little provocation in order to test the viability of any attack hypothesis, but were to take no main offensive action unless in-

structed to do so by Ren. The agent had a second-
ary purpose in leading an open move against
Magda—he hoped that news of it would tempt the
Imaiz to try and break out of Castle Di Guaard. He
had sufficient faith in the Pointed Tails to think
that Dion-daizan was unlikely to make his home-
ward journey alive.

Castle Magda was situated on the highest point
of Thirdhill, in a situation remote from the attendant township. It stood on a rocky plateau, three
parts of the extremeties of which gave way to
nothing but the slopes of a broken and inhospita-
ble hill. Working beneath the cover of the slopes,
the small and wiry commandos were split into
three groups, each with a local officer.

Ren alone, a known figure in the territory, felt
free to show himself openly. His presence on
Thirdhill could not be concealed during daylight
and he took advantage of this fact to make the
survey he needed to complete the assessments of
the high-level photographic data on Magda.

The intention had been that, having completed
his open evaluation of Magda's defense potential,
he would rejoin the commandos for a mock attack
to see what sort of response would be forthcoming
from the garrison in the absence of the Imaiz.
However, as he approached the main gatehouse
he was more than a little disturbed to find the
drawbridge down and the great gates open and
apparently unguarded. Intrigued by this phe-
nomenon, he ventured closer, the thought
crossing his mind that in the absence of the master
the attitude of the remaining garrison seemed to
be remarkably naive.

Or was it? If the Imaiz had left Magda, knowing
even a little of the threat on the plains, he might

have evacuated his whole garrison to safety. In which case Hardun's murder weapon would have been completely without success even if it had been fired. The idea seemed credible. If the Imaiz's strength resided mainly in the super-training of his bondforce, it would have been an unthinkable risk for him to have left them in the castle.

The chances were that the garrison was now dispersed around the township of Magda, waiting for the master to come and assure them it was safe to return. Wary of a trap, Ren returned to the commandos behind the ridge and used their radio to contact his own office. His servant took the call and dispatched a runner to contact Catuul Gras. Instead of sending a message, Catuul himself came to answer.

"Did you find anything, Tito?"

"Yes. As near as I can tell, Magda's been evacuated. Not even a token guard is posted. Are you perfectly sure the Imaiz is still bottled up in Castle Di Guaard?"

"Quite sure. Not even a rat could have got out of there unnoticed. We've had every inch of the walls under observation since the Imaiz went in. What had you in mind?"

"The occupation of Magda. I've some of Hardun's men with me. It would be quite a joke if, tired of waiting for the Imaiz to return, the garrison came back to find me in residence."

"Too risky," said Catuul gravely. "It's not like the Imaiz to leave the slightest thing to chance."

"He would scarcely have had time to make preparations once he realized what was going on."

"And what was going on?"

Ren realized that he had said too much. The Pointed Tails had not been given the probable reason why the *Imaiz* had found it so necessary to visit Di Guaard.

"We tricked him," said Ren obscurely. "That was why he left Magda. Risk it may be, but I'm going to try to get in there. I need to know what sort of facilities he has in Magda—and if we can manage to hold it, I think our battle's over. A lord dispossessed of his own castle won't find much following in Anharitte."

"Let me withdraw some Pointed Tails and try to locate the whereabouts of the garrison first."

"No. We don't have the time. And we daren't give the *Imaiz* the opportunity to escape from Di Guaard. You deal with the *Imaiz* and I'll try my luck with Magda. That way either or both of us has the chance to finish the fight for good."

Ren explained his proposition to the senior Rance commando. He too had independently formed the opinion that Magda was unoccupied and nodded a ready acceptance of Ren's idea. The men under him were battle-trained professionals, unused to sitting aside while a group of merchants and native warriors did the fighting for them. Whether or not Magda was defended, this was their chance to demonstrate what could uniquely be done by perfectly trained and equipped soldiery.

Ren was warned to take no part in the initial excursion. He saw the wisdom of this as the small, wiry commandos went expertly into action, almost melting into the background as they moved up toward the sinister towers of the castle. Every move they made was one of marvelous precision, each man knowing what area he had to cover with his firepower and what need not concern him until death took his neighbor. With the swift and deceptive mobility of lizards they moved up the main approaches. Some ventured onto the draw-bridge, some crossed it, others held careful reserve in the deadland beneath it. Each time they advanced they left nothing to chance. Had any resistance been offered it would at any time have found only a minimum of targets exposed.

Finally the whole force entered the gateway, having assured itself that the entry tunnel was safe. The last one to enter was the senior commando, who signaled to Ren that it was safe for him to follow. Ren moved up quickly, feeling a sudden loneliness and isolation now that the others were no longer visible. The whole affair had this far been conducted in silence, but now he became extraordinarily aware of just how absolute that silence was. He quickened his pace and had entered the long, dark tunnel of the entrance, expecting to find some of the commandos waiting for him and slightly perturbed to find that they were not. A nagging suspicion warned him that it had been far too easy. He was still telling himself this when the great portcullis gates fell at the ends of the tunnel, trapping him like a wild beast in a cage.

For his commando companions who had passed on into the inner ward the end was swift. A high-level stun bomb burst above their heads. Blastwise its effect was negligible, but its biological shock effect, caught and concentrated between the great walls of stone, was a disaster. All thirty-five Rance commandoes stiffened like posts and then crumpled to the ground. Those who had not been killed were severely concussed. Some of those who lived would be deaf for life. Others would have more or less permanent damage to the brain and other organs as a result of the shattering pressure and rarefaction of the stun bomb shockwave.

Caught in his cage, Ren was dealt agony. He held his hands over his screaming ears, though the blow at the pit of his stomach had been equally severe. Fortunately the narrow entrance to the tunnel and probably the gates themselves had protected him from all but a minor part of the shock. He rolled up and writhed on the dusty floor, oblivious to anything outside himself until some of the pain subsided. Then he climbed to his feet again, shaking his head to try and still the ringing in his ears and dimly thinking of escape. A brief examination of the portcullis, however, told him that his freedom, if gained, was going to have to be given by his captors. He could not arrange it for himself.

Through the heavy fret of the inner portcullis he could see the occupants of Magda beginning to emerge. Some began the task of sorting the dead commandos from the living. Others examined the fabric of the building's walls for any damage that might have resulted from the blast. Ren looked miserably out upon the scene and wondered when and what sort of attention would be paid to himself. He had his blaster under his tunic, but he was aware that to use it now could result only in his being destroyed like an unwanted dog. He might be able to make better use of its bargaining power in response to a more personal approach by his captors, but at this moment its function could be only a catalyst in an untidy and ignoble form of suicide.

Finally what looked like a medical team began directing the careful removal of those who might possibly be saved. Still no one paid any attention to Ren and, wondering if they even knew of his existence, he finally shouted to attract attention. Several of the slaves looked up and grinned in his direction. From this he deduced that his situation was known and that his incarceration was deliberate.

It was many hours later that the inner portcullis was raised, and he emerged from the dark recess of the tunnel to come blinking into the rays of the late-afternoon sun. Neither a vicious guard nor a firing squad awaited him. Instead a figure, peacock proud in a wealth of glorious fabrics, held out her hand in a reserved mode of welcome. And this he found equally daunting.

"Welcome to Magda, Agent Ren."

"Zinder—I—"

"You thought I was with Dion in Castle Di Guaard. Isn't that what you were going to say? To tell you the truth, we came back late last night."

"We? Dion-daizan too?" Ren felt impelled to ask the question, though he did not know why he expected an answer. He found her openness very disconcerting.

"And Barii." She was teasing him quietly. "There was quite a party on at Di Guaard last night. But we found it far too noisy. We left early."

"Damn!" Ren looked ruefully at the dust on his

shoes. "I must have at least three hundred men posted to stop you from leaving Firsthill. You people win every damn trick in the book. Did you know that was a crack Rance commando team you just destroyed? Competence is a tolerable sin, but omnipotence is a little out of fashion."

Zinder turned her head to survey the scene of the recent carnage in the courtyard.

"Not omnipotence, Agent Ren. Careful planning, good organization, fast communications, a sense of purpose and a modicum of luck. The usual ingredients needed to make a success of any major undertaking. We offer injury to those who try to injure us and ridicule for those who try to make us look ridiculous. We take an eye for a tooth and a life for an eye—and if that seems immoral, remember that the quarrel is not of our choosing."

Ren shrugged. "Then what do you intend to do with me?"

She was slightly amused. "I think we'll give you some supper and set you free again."

"I can't object to the arrangement, but the logic of it escapes me."

"Does it? If you were we, whom would you rather have as an enemy—yourself or the Butcher of Turais?"

"Butcher of Turias?"

"So they didn't tell even you! I'm not surprised. Alias Alek Hardun. He's a specialist in depopulating awkward places. The pogrom of Turais was only one of his accomplishments. It was no accident that he happened to have access to Rance toxin. And that's not a hundredth part of the mass-murder equipment he carries on that bloodwagon of his. Frankly we think that you and Director Vestevaal have been deceived into accepting him so easily. And either you stop him or we'll be forced to stop him ourselves. If Hardun comes out on top, even Roget could become another sparsely populated world."

"I can't accept that statement at its face value," said Ren. "But I know the director's worried about him and is trying to take some action."

"Trying's not enough. We were only able to stop Hardun below Di Guaard last night because we knew who he was and what he was capable of. But if he'd successfully destroyed Magda—who could have stopped him then? Can't you imagine the pattern? Here a lord goes crazy, and there another forgets to wake from hs sleep. Mutant rust decimates the harvest and the seat of central government is stricken by history's worst plague. Rance drafts in a thousand 'disaster relief experts' and, to shore a crumbling economy, appoints a puppet government. Then it's all over save the persecution and the exploitation."

"How much of this have you told Vestevaal?"

"All of it and more. I think he was convinced. But he has his own job to do also—and this we understand. He's a big man, your director—but I wonder if he's big enough to fight the combined weight of the merchant worlds. Only the Free Traders can contain them, but they're divided and doubtful and prone to manipulation themselves. But come! Dion will explain this far better than I. Though I think you'd better let me have your sword and your blaster before you meet him."

XIV

It was midnight as Ren started uncertainly back down the twisted Roads of Thirdhill. Zinder had taken his blaster, but had returned his sword at the gate, so that he had no fears for his own protection. His uncertainty arose from the wealth of damaging information. Dion-daizan had given him concerning Alek Hardun, the Butcher of Turais.

Ren had come to Magda full of certainty that he was indeed performing a necessary job. He now felt himself reduced to the status of a dupe and an unwitting accomplice of a trade-world cartel whose methods were becoming infamous throughout the universe. It made him wince to remember the number of times he had mentally applauded the news screen's announcements: *Disaster teams from Combien and Rance have been sent to the planet to offer immediate assistance* . . . Once those teams arrived, he knew now, the disasters multiplied and the need for assistance changed to one of enforced dependence.

On the other side of the coin, however, Hardun had warned Ren that the *Imaiz* would seek to divide his opposition and thereby ensure a continuance of his own schemes. This possible aspect of Dion's expert lecture had not been lost on Ren, though the documented evidence with which he had been presented was overwhelmingly in favor of the removal of Alek Hardun from the scene. Ren sensed that the *Imaiz* alone stood between Roget and the diabolical hands of Rance and her agents. With this in mind, he was not at all sure that his own plans to damage the *Imaiz* were still justified. He reflected that Vestevaal, having become convinced of the truth of the situation, had traveled immediately offworld to carry the battle directly to the powerful Free Trade Council. Of one thing Ren became certain—if he were again to have the strength of his own convictions, Alek Hardun and his murder ship must go.

Ahead of him, among the noises of the night, Ren heard a sound he knew. To the uninitiated it was the call of the nightbird. Ren knew it for the signal of the Pointed Tails. He answered it inexpertly and in a few moments Gras was at his side.

"What happened, Tito?" the scribe asked anxiously. "We had word that things went wrong at Magda and that you were captive."

"I was captive. But Dion-daizan decided to let me go again—I think because he likes the sporting nature of our opposition." Ren's sentence ended in heavy irony.

Catuul Gras looked at him as though transfixed by a blade.

"Dion-daizan in Magda? But he can't be—"

"He's there all right. So are Zinder and Barii. I've just taken supper with the three of them." A sudden anger overtook him. "Are they smaller than mice that they passed your watch at Di Guaard and were waiting to trap me when I arrived?"

In the dim light the scribe's expression was one of puzzlement followed by a sudden relaxation.

"Then you'll admit now that Dion's a wizard. It's not possible for anything to have escaped from Di Guaard without our knowing. Not only did we have the castle and the exits under surveillance, but we also had men on the routes and river crossings. If Dion reached Magda he must have flown like a bird."

The instant absurdity of the suggestion was soon overthrown by a new line of speculation in Ren's mind. "I wonder if you're right, Catuul. He couldn't have flown like a bird, but he could have flown nonetheless. In which direction was the wind last night?"

"There was not much wind, but the breeze persists from the southwest from now until the heavy weather breaks. Does that give you an idea?"

"I have a suspicion. Dion couldn't have used a conventional aircraft because you'd have heard the noise of engines. But if he'd had some sort of balloon available he could have used it in relative safety after nightfall. The natural winddrift would have carried them toward Thirdhill or at least into Magda province. And the river lights would have given them an indication of when it was safe to land."

"What's a balloon?" asked Catuul.

"A device that figures almost uniquely in ancient Terran history. It's a bag of gas or hot air—which is lighter than the air in which it floats. A big balloon can carry a basket containing several people. It could have lifted the three of them out of the Castle Di Guaard and if you weren't looking for it you'd never have seen it go. That way the

Imaiz could have escaped all your traps without resorting to wizardry. It only needs the application of a few physical principles and a bit of technical know-how."

"Wizardry or technical know-how, it's all the same to me," said Catuul. "What you call wizardry are the things that are done which are beyond the limits of what your education insists is possible. But the same applies to me. So the difference between our points of view is one of degree, not kind."

"Point taken, Catuul. But so far the *Imaiz* has done nothing beyond the comprehension of the average educated outworlder. This makes it reasonably certain that he's not a native of Roget, and various historical associations about his schemes strengthen my belief that he's a Terran."

The scribe was searching the darkness behind them, looking for something. Occasionally he would answer the low-pitched trade-calls that floated through the darkness. Finally he turned back to Ren and spoke.

"Hardun's men who were with you—weren't they released too?"

"No. All thirty-five were either killed or injured."

"I warned you it was dangerous." The scribe's face was grim. "The *Imaiz* never takes chances. And this fetches a point which we must settle between us, friend Tito. There was nothing in our contract about your carrying the fight using outworld soldiery. Nor about the use of longrange outworld weapons. If we were to place this fact before the Elders of the clans, they would relieve the Pointed Tails of any further obligations to you—nor would you obtain clan service elsewhere. The Elders would never consent to a clan's being party to any outworld scheme of aggression. I'm disappointed in you, Tito. I'd thought you understood us better."

Ren stopped walking and turned to face the scribe squarely.

"I do understand you and I admit I'm in error. But circumstances overtook me. Initially I was misled as to the reasons Alek Hardun came to Roget. He came under the guise of an advisor, but now appears to have independent operating status. By the time I was aware of this I found I had no power to stop him. The director has gone to the council to have the matter set to rights."

"Yet it was you who took the soldiers to Magda," objected Catuul.

"True. They were available and the exercise was intended purely as a reconnaissance. But when I believed Magda to be abandoned I thought that by one decisive move I might shorten the whole battle. That was a classic blunder that cost Doctor Hardun thirty-five men."

"I'd not have expected the price to be less." The scribe was critical. "Had the Imaiz not dealt with them—there are two hundred clansmen from all over the provinces around us now who would have made sure the Rance men never left Thirdhill."

"What?" Ren was aghast. "Do you really feel so strongly about them?"

"We may have our internal disputes in Anharitte, but armed outworld interference transcends any normal act of feud. Were it not so, even Roget could fall under some outworld yoke. Think about it, Tito. You'll see why it has to be so. And your part in this has been a cardinal transgression."

"I can't deny it. It's been a sad error both in judgment and in policy. Hardun's equipment and his tactics have become an embarrassment and were no part of my original intention. And I'm even more unhappy to have broken faith with your society."

"But in the light of today's expedition, how much reliance can we place on your word? Think carefully before you answer—I may yet have to speak for you to the Elders of the clans."

"The Elders must decide as they will. And you, too, Catuul. You know me better than most and must decide for yourself. My rejection of Alek Hardun is a personal inability to support his views on the cheapness of human life. I can't say otherwise even to save the spaceport or my job, which depends on it."

"That's precisely what I wanted to hear," said the scribe. "But I've been less frank with you. The Elders have already discussed the matter in council. They gave two decisions. The first is that all society services will be withdrawn from outworlders until Hardun and his ship have been removed—"

"And the second?"

"That you were to be killed unless I personally was satisfied with your intention and your integrity."

"And have you come to that decision?" Ren felt his sword hang heavy at his side.

"Of course." Catuul's smile broadened in the

dim light from the night sky. "Or you would have
been dead within minutes of leaving Castle
Magda. Come, friend Tito, we have your
cushion-craft waiting on the far side of the crossing."

"All thirty-five men?" Hardun's voice reached
the peak of incredulity.

"It wouldn't have mattered if they had been a
hundred," said Ren. "The *Imaiz* is more than a
match for anything you can put up. Frankly, your
tactics have become a liability. I've sent a spacegram to the Free Trade Council expressing the
opinion that if you're allowed to remain on Roget
the spaceport facility will certainly be lost."

"You did what?" Hardun's new peak of disbelief was suddenly tempered by relief. "Now I
know you're joking, Tito. I see copies of every
spacegram transmitted from here. I know damn
well you've sent no such thing."

"You used to see copies," corrected Ren. "The
Free Trade Council has already instructed the
spaceport staff not to cooperate with you and
they're leaning heavily on Rance to have you
pulled out. I know of this because I held a personal conversation with the director at Free Trade
Central. And you won't receive a recording of that
either. He confirmed everything I'd learned about
the Butcher of Turais."

"Turais? That old propaganda line—" Hardun
was vehement. "If you'd believe that you'd believe anything."

"I would believe anything about you, Alek.
That's why I complained to the council. The
urgency of your removal can't be overstressed.

They're to hold a debate on it. I imagine the result will be to apply some tough sanctions against Rance until they're forced to order you out. I don't imagine that'll make you very popular with your masters, either. So I'm advising you now to get offworld before the storm really breaks."

"I'll see you in hell first, Tito. I wouldn't dream of moving a centimeter unless I get specific instructions from Rance Politico."

"Very conformative. But I wasn't asking you to go—I was warning you not to stay. Your departure is imminent. Either you decamp of your own volition or run the very probable risk of being removed perhaps violently by someone like the Imaiz. And if that happens Rance will be spared much loss of face—so I don't imagine they'll grieve unduly."

"The risk is negligible. It's a complete certainty there's nothing at Roget that can harm an armed battle cruiser at dock."

"I don't share your certainty. The societies have withdrawn all services until your ship has been removed. The Imaiz not only has no opposition but can probably acquire substantial assistance if he requires it. And I don't think Di Irons is going to miss the point for very long—in which case the planetary government will also be involved. So the opposition ranged against you runs from Dion-daizan through the Free Trade Council up to possible intervention by the Galactic Federation. If you get offworld now you might just about save your own skin."

"You're either a brave man or a complete fool," said Hardun savagely. "I've killed men before for offering a whole lot less provocation. Your outlook's so far adrift from the realities of galactic life that you're really too pathetic to be true."

"I've been around, Alek. And wherever I've been I've looked in depth as well as at the surface. It's not a perspective you'd understand but it means I can back my judgment against yours with a reasonable chance of being right."

Ren turned on his heel and stalked out of the room. It was obvious that his attempt to persuade Hardun to go voluntarily had met with no sort of success. Ren's knowledge of spaceport security measures—and of the detection and defense capabilities of a docked battle cruiser—did not incline him to place much faith in the idea that the Imaiz would have a greater success by his own methods. They would probably have to wait until the pressure on Rance brought about an official recall. Ren shuddered. In the meantime Hardun could act without restriction—and if he accepted that his period of opportunity was limited, the next twenty-four hours could be a very crucial time in Anharitte's history.

It might have been his imagination affecting his interpretation of the scene or it might have been some social reflection of the societies' decision, but Ren had the distinct impression of unease in the city as he returned. The markets were quiet, almost deserted. The streets were far less crowded than usual and his own office was deserted and dead. His bondservants had been withdrawn by the Pointed Tails—whose legal property they were—and the normally busy household was at a standstill. Ren was even forced into the extreme of doing his own shopping when he wished to eat—and the preparation of his solitary meal was a process which caused him to think seriously about his next move.

He could not back down on his stand against Hardun nor could he reasonably do more than he had done to secure the latter's departure. There appeared to be no basis for any sort of pact with the *Imaiz* that would not be compromising later—and in any case Ren felt that he had nothing of interest to offer. The best mode of release from the impasse would undoubtedly be the swift intervention by the Free Trade Council acting on Rance. Ren could only hope that the council would successfully act before Di Irons began to examine too closely the reasons behind the Pointed Tails' decision to withdraw their services. If the prefect were to learn the truth about the rocket launcher on the plains he would have no option but to start a chain of protests that must involve the planetary government and ultimately the Galactic Federation itself.

Di Irons, then, was the main problem for the moment. Idly Ren speculated on the strategy for a successful pattern of bluff if the prefect's sure nose for trouble should lead him too close to the truth. The answers were not encouraging. He therefore decided that this would be a prudent time to visit some of the more distant of the company's trading installations. By this ruse he could probably delay a confrontation until the removal of Alek Hardun was an accomplished fact. Accordingly he packed in preparation for an early start and retired exhausted to his bed.

An explosion—or rather a series of explosions—broke him savagely out of his sleep. He awoke in alarm as multiple flashes of light glared in window-patterned squares of whiteness from the walls of his room. The thunder followed swiftly. Ren leaned back prepared to listen to the storm—until it slowly filtered into his consciousness that there was no such thing as a storm on Roget.

In an instant of panic he flung himself from his bed and put his head out of the window. The night sky was ringing as yet another great explosion from the direction of the plains shredded the unwilling air. Without pausing to dress Ren ran downstairs to the microwave communicator. As he turned on the stair the largest explosion yet made the building vibrate. Only the distance in the quality of the sound made him certain that the explosion was at the spaceport. The nature and effect of so violent a blast at that point of origin was something he scarcely dared to consider.

Although he called both on the service and emergency frequencies, he could obtain no reply from the spaceport control. This silence was unprecedented and suggested a state of crisis so acute that even the information backup for the Disaster Center was unobtainable. This convincingly fitted the scale of the catastrophe he had deduced from the intensity of the shockwaves. It was credible that as much as a quarter of the spaceport installation had been destroyed. On an undeveloped world like Roget where civil emergency services were virtually nonexistent, the entire work of disaster containment and rescue work would have to be handled by the spaceport's own personnel.

Ren dressed hurriedly. He did not even need

light in his rooms. The sky, made bright by the angry redness of a major spaceport fire, provided more than adequate illumination. Knowing that his training would enable him to do little in the way of offering practical assistance, his intention on reaching the street door had been merely to walk to the limits of Firsthill in order to gain a better view. As he descended the steps, however, two armed watchmen flung themselves hurriedly across his path.

"Agent Ren you're not permitted to leave."

"What do you mean?"

"Prefect Di Irons' orders. You're to be confined to your chambers until he's free to deal with you."

"But why the hell? This is no doing of mine."

"That you must discuss with him. But you'd better be convincing. Nights such as this were never known in Anharitte before you made trouble with the Imaiz."

Ren allowed himself to be escorted back into the chambers, where the watchmen maintained an uncommunicative guard. When the light of the morning was well advanced, he heard other noises in the house and soon guessed that his bondservants had been returned and were picking up their duties as though no interruption of service had occurred. Shortly his breakfast tray was placed before him. His guards were completely ignored.

By such signs he knew that Alek Hardun had been wrong in his certainty that no force on Roget was capable of dealing with an armed space cruiser at dock. It was a fair bet that about a third of the spaceport installation had gone with it. By

some ingenious piece of wizardry a way had been
found through all the alarms and defenses and the
Imaiz had made good his promise.

An hour after mid-day the unusual echo of
horses' hoofs clattered to the door of his chambers. The sound was rare because the great horses
of Roget, fully as large as the ancient Terran
dray-horses, were unpopular beasts on the
crowded roads of the city. They had their place at
the great provincial estates but for town work they
were used mainly by the civil powers as a symbol
of authority. A message from Di Irons required
Ren to join the cavalcade to the spaceport. The
reins of the great saddled and bridled beast were
flung toward him with the instruction that he was
to mount.

Ren's riding experience was little and the size
of his steed was daunting. He said as much, but
his protests were dismissed.

"Then here's your chance to learn Agent. The
prefect won't wait."

Somehow he managed to mount. He sat unhappily astride the great beast whose back seemed as
broad and as warm as the bed Ren had vacated
during the night. Having mastered the art of stay-
ing on top of the moving animal, he next faced the
problem of control. He found himself assisted by
the fact that the giant horse appeared to know
exactly what was required of it in terms of destination and speed. It obediently followed the messenger and two others through the streets of
Firsthill, out on to the Trade Road, down the
slopes and on to the Via Arena.

The messenger rode hard, without pausing for

further explanation. The fact that his escort rode mainly ahead of him led Ren to suspect that his presence was required for a constructive purpose rather than a punitive one. They soon came in sight of the spaceport, from which, even in daylight, the bright flames from burning fuel tanks showed crimson under the vast columns of smoke.

Ren's initial surprise at being conveyed in so unusual a manner was soon dispelled as he realized that carriage by the giant horses were certainly the fastest means of transport available. Although cushion-craft were able to produce a better turn of speed on the open stretch of the Via Arena, the slower working of the craft in the city gave ample advantage to horses. His present journey was accomplished in well under half an hour. Bruised and sore, Ren clung frantically to the saddle horn and only fell when he attempted to dismount.

XV

Di Irons, looking fiercer and sterner than ever, waited for Ren to pick himself out of the dust, then strode away, indicating that the agent should follow. Ren followed painfully, wondering if his encounter with the horse had done something irrevocable to his legs. Their path took them broadly across the spaceport, most of which was obscured by wide trails of drifting smoke. The prefect stopped when finally they neared the number-five landing bowl where the Rance battle cruiser had been.

Ren caught his breath as the scale of the catastrophe became apparent. The tall ship had been totally demolished and the parts further shattered. Even the single components seemed destroyed. Only a very small part of the ship's total mass was still evident. The rest of it had presumably been vaporized or dispersed over many thousands of meters of terrain. Even the nearly indestructible wolframic of the landing bowl was heavily cratered as though from a major war. The picture was one of violence multipled by violence. It was a job most thoroughly done.

"How did it happen?" asked Ren.

Di Irons put on a thunderous scowl. "Pictor Don has a theory that the ship was toppled by an s.h.e.

charge placed in the vicinity of one of the ship's stabilizers. Her engines then exploded and that touched off her magazine. Unfortunately she was heavily overarmed and some of the later explosions took away a fair proportion of the spaceport buildings. I've no doubt we'll be receiving a detailed account of the damage from the spaceport Disaster Control center in due course. That's why I wanted you here. You're going to give me an independent view of how it was done, who did it—and why it was necessary."

"Me? But I know nothing about it. I was asleep at the time."

"That's no excuse," said Di Irons. "I'll wager you know a great deal about it. Pretense will save you nothing. Let's be in no doubt as to where you stand. In the past twenty-five hours I've uncovered sufficient facts about you and the activities with which you've been involved to have you declared *persona non grata* on just about every civilized planet in the universe. Not only that, but for default of various laws on Roget under Space Conventions I could encourage our government to make claim for damages that would not only bankrupt your Company but would cripple another half-dozen of their Free Trade associates.

"Having warned you to follow the advice of your society on how to conduct a feud with the *Imaiz*, you have no conceivable defense for your actions. So do you now volunteer to answer my questions or do I have to break both you and the Company?"

"What exactly do you want to know?" asked Ren unhappily.

"This battle cruiser—it must have carried

enough armaments to start a major war. Was it put here by the Free Trade Council?"

"No. It was donated by Rance, ostensibly as a technical backup facility. I don't think the majority of the council was aware that it was anything else."

"So why did it possess a fully equipped war potential?"

"It was one of Rance's so-called 'disaster ships'—though I've come to suspect that their function is to cause disasters not to alleviate them."

"Didn't you know of this when you asked for it?"

"I didn't ask for it. It just arrived. When I found out what sort of equipment it carried I complained to Director Vestevaal. He went immediately to Free Trade Central to demand its withdrawal."

"Hmmm!" Di Irons nodded thoughtfully. "And I take it that somebody couldn't wait to see it go peacefully. Your friend the *Imaiz*, perhaps?"

"It's no evidence," said Ren. "But he knew it for what it was and its demolition has a characteristic thoroughness."

"That's agreed," said Di Irons, looking around at the widespread damage. "And in the circumstances I don't think we shall hear much from Rance about her loss, especially if Director Vestevaal's already protesting about it at Free Trade Central. But more than the ship went here. A lot of highly valuable spaceport installation went with it. When the Galactic Spaceports commission learns of it, the repercussions are going to be grave. I'm going to be under pressure to produce some good answers. Frankly, I don't have the expertise in outworld technology to produce those answers. But you do. And you've the additional advantage of knowing both the *Imaiz* and the pattern of life in Anharitte, neither of which an outworld investigator would know. Therefore I'm willing to strike a bargain with you."

"What sort of bargain?"

"We both suspect it was the *Imaiz* who destroyed this ship. I want to know how much evidence against the *Imaiz* could be gathered by an outworld inquiry into the disaster."

"You choose your words most carefully, Prefect."

"In this instance I've a good reason to do so."

"And what have I to gain from the exercise?"

"Give me some good answers, Ren, and I might forget to file any charges against yourself or the Company."

"I'll willingly try, though your terms don't give me much option. But I'll need information. How cooperative can I expect to find the spaceport staff?"

"They themselves are in default for permitting an armed warcraft to remain docked at their facility beyond the recognized refueling time. Therefore their careers are equally in my hands. I suspect you'll find them very cooperative indeed."

Pictor Don, the spaceport's emergency commander, spread his hands resignedly.

"I can assure you, Tito, that outside sabotage is quite out of the question. Nobody could have gotten through without detection. Because of the permanent danger to personnel around the landing bowls, the whole area is monitored by radar.

The radar overscan extends well beyond the spaceport perimeter. The computer constantly oversees all activity in the area and throws up alarm signals for any potentially dangerous or unusual event."

"What other defenses have you?"

"Mainly the fences. The first and second fences form a corridor manned by a patrol with guard dogs. Then there's an electrified fence inside that and the inner one's a barbed barrier. It would take a very clever person indeed to get through that lot."

"We happen to suspect a very clever person. What I'm trying to establish is—did he indeed get through or was the blast an accident? What about the gates?"

"Only two—both remotely controlled and responding only to the controller's direct orders. He has to satisfy himself by computer verification of ident cards and the vision link that the person asking for admission has the necessary authority to enter."

"And did he give clearance to anyone at a time reasonably close to the blowup?"

"No. There were no admissions for at least four hours before the blowup occurred."

"Then it would have to be through the fence. Has the whole perimeter been checked?"

"Electrical checks have been carried out. Nothing was found. Physical examination of all the wire on the perimeter will take a little time."

"Then let me have the answers as soon as you can," said Ren. "If somebody penetrated that fence, I want to know how. Did your radar scan tell you nothing?"

"The watch computer signaled nothing unusual."

"How critical is the watch computer?"

"Sufficient for normal purposes."

"But does it discriminate between different types of radar returns?"

"Necessarily so. Frequently animals from the plains stray near to the outer fence and trigger a minor alert. Also some birds and small animals actually live out on the bowls. The computer has been programmed to reject the movement of small creatures and to respond mainly to the approach of something the size of a cushion-craft or one of the tracked tenders."

"Then how does it function for personnel protection on the bowls?"

"It's spectrum filtered to give maximum response to metallic objects while remaining relatively insensitive to organics and nonmetals. Any crews working on the bowls will naturally be wearing thermo-reflective suits and these give a very good radar return."

"So it is possible for an unsuited man to have walked across the bowls without the computer's classifying him as an object to be reported?"

"It's possible, but I see the point as rather academic. Nobody could damage a battle cruiser with less than about a hundred kilos of s.h.e. explosive. I'd seriously doubt that somebody broke the fence and carried that weight across the bowls on foot. Perhaps a trained man might do it—but I don't believe it happened. I think they'd have to use a vehicle—and if they'd done so the computer would have spotted it and sounded the alarm."

"Nevertheless," said Ren, "I'd like to know if there was anything on the radar scan below the computer's indicating threshold. Do you tape a record?"

"Of course." Pictor Don shrugged his shoulders. "I'll have a replay set up in the operations room. If you want my opinion—it's a waste of time."

"What are you looking for, Ren?" The stern and thoughtful prefect was shadowing Ren closely, listening to every syllable of his investigation. "I'd have thought Don's evidence that there was no penetration of the fence was pretty conclusive."

"Not conclusive enough. If it did happen we need to know now, not have it thrown up during some outworld inquiry. All defenders and all defense systems have blind spots. If someone has the wit and the ability to figure just where these blind spots are, they form a positive advantage to the attacker. A bit of ingenuity coupled with the right know-how should produce a method of attack the defenders won't expect because they know it to be impossible. Our prime suspect in this case is a recognized master of impossible events and is also a considerable technician. I can't see that dogs, a few wire fences and a radar scan need be any deterrent to the *Imaiz*."

"There's been some talk of rockets," said Di Irons. "Couldn't Dion have used one without having to penetrate the fence?"

"He may well have the capability at Magda, but that wasn't the way it was done. As I see the evidence, the ship was toppled, as you've already said, by an s.h.e. charge placed under a stabilizer.

But that couldn't in itself have initiated the entire chain of disasters that followed. Almost certainly the ship was toppled upon a further line of explosive charges, and the direction of the ship's fall was calculated to insure that those charges would do the maximum damage. It was an exercise in fine mathematics, undertaken by someone who had a very clear idea of the working layout of such a battle cruiser."

"From which you conclude?"

"That the operation was carried out by a competent outworlder—someone familiar with space constructions. And it would have taken time and careful measurement to place those charges accurately. Whoever did it must have worked on the bowl under cover of darkness and had a pretty shrewd idea that he would not be picked up by the radar monitor. That's an assembly of knowledge and skills very difficult to match. I think that Dion must be a well-trained saboteur—in addition to his other talents."

Di Irons was not yet convinced.

"If I understand Pictor Don correctly it would have taken at least a hundred kilos of explosive just to topple the ship. If you're now saying that further charges were laid—they must add up to a considerable extra weight of explosive. All this had to be moved through the fence and brought across at least half a kilometer of landing bowls—without detection."

"I know very little about explosives," said Ren. "But I'd doubt that less than two hundred kilos of s.h.e. would have done the trick."

"And brought in without using a vehicle? Do

you suppose they used mules or magic?" The prefect was sarcastic.

"I don't know how it was done, but I'm willing to bet we'll find a few answers on the below-threshold level of the radar records."

The radar overscan, untrimmed by the computer, reflected considerable movement of wildlife outside the perimeter fence. The false alarms would have been continual had not spectrum filtering been employed. In contrast, the casual movements of spaceport personnel and vehicles were easily distinguishable by the heightened radar responses to the various metallic substances they carried. It was at about this level of discrimination that the computer operated.

Pictor Don replayed the scan at its original speed for the two hours prior to the blowup. He and Ren concentrated fully on the unedited replay screen, while Di Irons fretted in the background, unable to comprehend the screen's symbolism. All of the first hour of the replay and half of the second passed without producing any information of obvious interest. Suddenly Ren gave a cry.

"Southeast corner—behind the shadow of the freighter on pad eight—something is moving on the bowls."

There was no doubt of the fact. Emerging from the radar shadow of the freighter, already within the wire, two images sped across the bowls toward the doomed ship. The radar responses were weak, well below the computer's preset threshold. The moving forms gave no clue as to their form or composition. Pictor Don ran marker blips across the screen to measure the velocity of the moving points. He frowned at the resulting calculation.

"Slightly up on fifteen kilometers an hour," he said in puzzlement. "Men running perhaps, but certainly not men carrying two hundred kilos of deadweight."

"Perhaps horses?" asked Di Irons.

Don shook his head. "Not enough mass for horses."

"Is there much metal present?" asked Ren.

"Some, but its not very distinct. More like a grid than a solid. Certainly not enough mass to be a vehicle. The computer wouldn't be able to distinguish between it and the oxide glaze on the bowls themselves."

"Then what the devil can have carried them across the field at a speed like that?"

"Did you ever think of wizardry?" Di Irons had the faintest smile of mischief around his grizzled mouth.

"I don't care for wizardry," said Ren. "There's a physical explanation for all this. Dion-daizan's no more of a wizard than I am."

In less than three minutes the two dots had moved from the perimeter across the intervening half kilometer to the foot of the threatened Rance ship. Their passage must have been effectively silent—they appeared to make no effort to avoid the lock-watch who would have been aroused by the sound of an approaching vehicle.

"Were they invisible also?" asked Di Irons.

When the dots stopped under the radar shadow of the ship, the screen picture became confused by the sheer mass against which the returns were being measured. In less than a minute, however, the dots separated themselves and streaked back toward the perimeter fence, moving even faster than before. Soon they were lost behind the shadow of the freighter on pad eight and the scene closed down to an apparent stillness as the time approached the moment of blowup.

"Well, we still don't know what got in, but at least we know where," said Ren. "Let's go and take a closer look."

On the southeast perimeter, where the bulk of the freighter on pad eight stood squarely between them and the damaged radar tower, Ren examined the wire. There was little wonder the break had not been detected before. Had he not had a suspicion of what to look for, he would not have found it for himself. The wires had been cut to a level sufficient to admit something not much larger than a man. Every single strand had subsequently been neatly butt-welded to form a virtually invisible repair. Any competent technician could have done it—given the right equipment and the necessary time.

"But we had guard-dog patrols between the outer fences," objected Pictor Don, when the fact was pointed out.

"Who mans the patrols?" asked Ren.

"One of the so-called societies—very reliable."

"Perhaps! But for most of the night there was a withdrawal of society services from all matters affecting outworlders. In effect, there was a period when the *Imaiz* could move unopposed on whatever course he chose. He might even have been able to enlist society aid. I'm reasonably certain that if he chose to cut these wires last night, the dogs would have been conveniently elsewhere."

"But why should the societies cooperate with him in this way?" Pictor Don was perplexed.

"Because," said Ren, "Dion's probably the only force standing between Roget as it is—and eventual domination by Rance. I know this. The societies know it and I suspect my Lord Di Irons knows it also. I may be an outworlder, but I've heard enough about Rance's mailed fist in the universe to know that, given a free choice, I would have been out there last night holding that wire open for Dion to enter."

Ren turned away from the wire and wandered into the scrub edging the surrounding plain. Shortly he came back and addressed Di Irons.

"Well, Prefect, I'm ready to answer your questions."

Di Irons compressed his mouth under his beard. The eyes that met Ren's were full of comprehension, edged with a slight smile.

"What about that radar record?" asked the Prefect.

"What radar record? It must have been destroyed in the blowup."

"And the wire?"

"Could never have been disturbed. Technology on Roget obviously isn't far enough advanced to permit a gas-shielded electric butt-weld to be made."

"And the blowup?"

"Who knows," said Ren. "Accidents can always happen on an overarmed man-of-war. I think the point should be made most strongly to the Spaceports Commission. They must be encouraged to take far greater care of ships when operating on foreign soil. Otherwise it might prove inconvenient to have a spaceport so near Anharitte."

"And we can positively rule out outside intervention?"

"I can think of no way in which a man or perhaps two men with neither beast nor vehicle could travel half a kilometer in three minutes with at least two hundred kilos of dead weight. Such an idea smacks of wizardry."

"Which we all know doesn't exist," said Di Irons. "You know, Tito, I've a feeling I've misjudged you. You've a depth of perception I would not have associated with your mercenary profession. My report will follow the lines of your summary—and you and Pictor Don can sign a testimony to its accuracy. You've proven to me that there could have been no outside intervention. But strictly off the record—and since you don't admit Dion's a wizard—how do you imagine the thing could have been done?"

Ren nodded and turned out towards the brush.

"Come over here. Do you see those marks in the dust? What do you suppose made those?"

"That's very strange. I don't think I've seen the like of them before. Do you suppose snakes—"

"I imagine they're snake tracks," said Ren, tongue in cheek. "But they bear a strong resemblance to the tracks of a device I once saw used on Terra."

Di Irons straightened as a society runner approached. The man had come around the perimeter from the gate to hand him a message form. The fellow's exertions underscored the urgency with which he had been dispatched. The prefect scanned the paper anxiously and handed it to

Pictor Don. Both men seemed tremendously upset.

"Trouble?" asked Ren.

The form was passed to him. With mounting disbelief he read the message.

TRANSGALACTIC NEWSFAX(:) RANCE SPOKESMEN HAVE REVEALED THAT IN ORDER TO CONTAIN WIDESPREAD CIVIL DISORDER ON ROGET ESPECIALLY ANHARITTE THEY ARE DISPATCHING THIRTY DISASTER SHIPS IMMEDIATELY(:) ANHARITTE SPACEPORT HAS ALREADY BEEN ATTACKED BY RIOTERS AND A RANCE GOODWILL SHIP DESTROYED(:) THE CIVIL GOVERNMENT IS NOW REPORTED POWERLESS TO COUNTER INSURRECTION(:) FIRST TASK OF RANCE DISASTER TEAMS WILL BE TO ESTABLISH CIVIL ORDER AND TO REMAIN IN CONTROL UNTIL DEMOCRATIC LIBERTY IS REESTABLISHED(:) MESSAGE ENDS(:)

"Get me an FTL communications link with Free Trade Central," said Ren angrily when he had absorbed the shock. "I'll get the director to blow this scheme apart right from the top—at Galactic Federation Headquarters if necessary."

"That may not be easy," said Pictor Don unhappily. "Our FTL link to anywhere is routed through the relay terminal on Rance."

"Damn!" Ren looked across the blasted spaceport where even now the smoke trails persisted over the scene of devastation. The enormity of Rance's fabrication made his head spin, but his heart was seized with the cold clamp of fear.

If Alek Hardun's murder wagon had been regarded as a goodwill vessel, Ren hated to think what thirty openly operating disaster ships would bring. Despite his increasing respect for the resourceful Dion-daizan he knew that salvation this time depended on the rapid acquisition of an armed spacefleet. Presumably not even the wizard of Anharitte could produce that. Or could he? At the moment Ren knew only from the trackmarks in the dust that the *Imaiz* possessed at least two bicycles.

XVI

The sky was beginning to darken with the approach of rain as Ren returned from the spaceport. The sullen, brooding clouds fitted his mood. Di Irons had offered him a horse but, still sore from his last encounter with one of these magnificent beasts, Ren had declined. Nor had he accepted Pictor Don's offer of the loan of a cushion-craft. More than anything Ren wanted to be alone. He needed time to think.

Rance was preparing to put down on Roget some thirty so-called disaster teams, ostensibly to establish order in a situation where factually no assistance was required. But once their ships had landed, Ren had no doubt, a sequence of "disasters" would occur to justify Rance's continued occupation of the planet. Rance would claim her actions were selfless and humane. Under the propaganda, however, lurked the harsh realities of conquest and exploitation—the real reasons behind the expedition.

The preservation of planetary independence was a fundamental right guaranteed by the charter of the Galactic Federation. A competent spacefleet was maintained to give teeth to the Federation's resolutions. The problem was therefore one of communication. Only FTL transmitters had the capability of communicating in real time with the Federation before Rance's occupation became part of history. Because of the interstellar distances involved, Roget's FTL transmitter, located at the spaceport, was routed through the relay terminal on Rance itself.

It was certainly no accident that Ren's call to Free Trade Central had been unable to gain a communication channel. The Rance relay had not even bothered to reply. Presumably Rance was already claiming that the communications failure was due to civil disruption on Roget. Nothing could be farther from reality, but Ren, shorn of the ability to broadcast the truth across the universe, could only fret with frustration and anxiety under the leaden sky of Anharitte.

The ships of Rance would probably appear in Roget's orbit within two weeks. The "disasters" would follow as an aftermath, rather than as a prelude to their coming. His experience with Alek Hardun had taught Ren what to expect. A silent dusting with mutagens would ensure the warping of the harvests. Virulent plagues would decimate the populations of the cities. Afterward would come the terrors of the persecutions as the "saviors" from Rance sought out the "transgressors" of Roget. Finally another planet would be added to the sad, mute colonies of the trade worlds.

Ren wondered if Director Vestevaal would guess the truth of the situation and whether, having guessed, he could carry his convictions with sufficient force to bring the fleet arm of the Federation into action. Certainly his claims would need substantiation if they were to hold against the barrage of propaganda from Combien and Rance.

With these preoccupations in his mind Ren had reached the Black Rock before the coming of the rain drew his attention to his own predicament. He shrugged, drew up his collar and turned his face skyward, the better to appreciate the refreshing nature of the shower. Suddenly aware of himself, he was intrigued to find that he had walked the major length of the Via Arena without being consciously aware of a step he had taken.

The stalls and boutiques beyond the Arena were mainly closed. With characteristic logic the *Ahhn* had seen no point in keeping regular trade hours at a time when bad weather rendered customers unlikely. Ren walked between the sheeted hutments and stalls, feeling that the members of such an independent race were unlikely easily to accept domination by Rance. Certainly they deserved a better fate. He wished it were within his power to secure it for them.

Where the route to Magda Crossing met the Trade Road he stopped, looking toward the dark mass of Thirdhill. He wondered if Dion-daizan had become aware of Rance's action and what, if anything, the wizard could do about it. Slightly beyond his line of sight the dark castle nestled somewhere on the hill, guarding a range of secrets that appeared to cover a broader spectrum with their every exercise. Was it impossible, Ren asked himself, that the *Imaiz* had an answer even to this problem? The idea did not carry a great deal of conviction. The *Imaiz* was a minor lord of a minor province on a relatively undeveloped world. He would need to be a mighty wizard indeed to take on the armed might of Rance.

Nevertheless the faint hope persisted. It took Ren away from his own route and down to the water's edge. The rain, now drifting in sheets, lost him the stretch of Firstwater in a cloud of drizzle. At Magda Crossing no ferries were available. The fragile slimboats had been drawn up under cover and the ferrymen had gone. Typical *Ahhn* logic dictated that nobody but a fool or a felon would be traveling in weather such as this. Ren searched the bank for a quarter of an hour but could not find anybody to take him across and he could not have handled a slimboat by himself against the

Finally the rain began to penetrate his clothing and hang cold around his neck and shoulders. Fearing a chill in this land of inadequate medicine, Ren retraced his steps away from the river and climbed the slopes of the Trade Road. When he finally reached his office chambers he was soaked to the skin, thoroughly exhausted and depressed. Such was his condition that his servants were alarmed and insisted that he bathe immediately, then retire to bed.

He was halfway to acceding to their wishes when a thought struck him. His office computing terminal had not been used since the discovery of the line tap. The line had been disconnected at the spaceport in order to deny Dion-daizan unauthorized access to the computer data banks, but Ren could not recollect whether the tap itself had been broken. Experimentally he took the cover from the keyboard and sat before the instrument. As he keyed his call sign the board responded with a ready acknowledgment.

REN CALLING MAGDA.

MAGDA ACKNOWLEDGES. PLEASE PRO-
CEED.

RANCE SENDING THIRTY DISASTER SHIPS
TO ROGET. COMMUNICATIONS LINK WITH
OUTWORLD BROKEN BY RANCE COM-
TERMINAL. THOUGHT YOU OUGHT TO
KNOW.

MESSAGE RECIEVED AND UNDERSTOOD.
DION WILL BE INFORMED. TRANSMISSION
ENDS.

As the lights died on the board Ren felt possessed of a sudden chill and began to tremble
violently. Afraid for him, his servants insistently
dragged him away from the terminal and stripped
the wet clothes from his back.

Their concern proved justified. On the following morning he awoke with a fever, and pains ran
through every muscle of his body. A physician
from the Pointed Tails arrived and made him
drink a pungent brew of herbs—it cooled the fever
but did nothing for the aches that troubled him
whichever way he lay. Fully twelve days passed
before he recovered sufficiently to continue with
his business.

On the fourteenth day the microwave communicator brought him an urgent message from
San Weba, the spaceport controller.

"Tito, our scanners have just picked up a fleet of
vessels about a hundred diameters out. At a guess
I'd say they are the Rance disaster fleet. They're
keeping radio silence and refuse to communi-
cate."

"Thanks," said Ren. "I'll pass the message to Di
Irons. He'll probably send a messenger to the

planetary government. If the fellow takes a fast horse he might even reach his destination before the battle is lost. Had any luck with the FTL relay?"

"Rance refuses to answer us and we don't have enough power to reach another relay station. Rance has even stopped transmitting galactic newsfax items to us. We're effectively isolated from the rest of the galaxy until Rance decides it's safe to lift the lid again."

"By which time those of us who know the score aren't likely to be around. The destruction of the spaceport was one of the first 'incidents' dreamed up by Rance, because they have to pretend it was our communications link that failed. But as soon as their ships get through they may try to turn the myth into a reality. I think they'll hit the spaceport first—and hit it hard. Wouldn't it be wise to evacuate just in case?"

"We've been discussing that, Tito. The general feeling is against it. We've broken the FTL transmitter away from its relay beam path and are using a scanner in the hope we can contact a stellar cruiser and get a message through to the Federation."

"It's worth a try, San," said Ren. "Though the possibilities of a stellar cruiser just happening to come within beam range are pretty slim."

He broke contact and called for a runner to take a message to Di Irons.

An hour later there was another call from San Weba. This time the controller's words were edged with excitement.

"Tito, something's happening. Can you get down here fast?"

"What's the panic?"

"Ships, dozens of them, coming from all sides. They can't all be from Rance."

Ren needed no further invitation. Without one of Di Irons' horses the quickest method of reaching the spaceport was by cushion-craft, despite the slow poling to the city limits. He speculated on the possibility of taking the cushion-craft down the Trade Road without waiting for stavebearers. Though such practice was illegal, he suspected Di Irons would be lenient in view of the circumstances. He realized, however, that he had a more than even chance of wrecking the craft and killing himself if he lost control on the slopes and had to deflate the cushion while at speed. Reluctantly he called for a stave team and went down the Trade Road in the slower, more orthodox manner.

Fortune was kind to him. No oxcarts or similar vehicles got in his way. The stavebearers responded to his urgency and ran consistently fast, using their poles only when guidance was absolutely necessary. Once past the Black Rock he was able to open up to full speed and the dust from the start of his passage along the Via Arena could scarcely have settled before he reached the spaceport entrance.

The gates were wide open. Normal details of security and procedure had been abandoned. Ren slammed the cushion-craft straight across the empty landing bowls toward the control center and was running through the door before the air cushion had time to drop the craft's shell to the ground.

Inside the traffic-control room everyone was

gathered around the screens. San Weba saw Ren come in and beckoned him through the crowd of technicians and spaceport personnel. He pointed to the main detector screens on which the state of activity in the spacefield around Roget was represented by dozens of slowly moving points of light.

"You see that cluster there, Tito—they're the ones we saw first. There are about thirty of them—we assume them to be the disaster ships from Rance. But these—" his fingers raked over fully a hundred widespread points of light on the screen—"I don't know what they are or where they came from. They must have dropped out of spacewarp well within our beam range."

Ren was disbelieving. "They couldn't have dropped out of warp that close."

"But they did. Some must have dropped out within two planetary diameters. I've never heard of such pinpoint accuracy before. Nor of anyone prepared to take the risk. If a commercial freight outfit could learn to do that they could save themselves a week on every trip."

"Then these are obviously not a commercial outfit. And if Rance had that capability her ships would have been here a week ago. I think what we may be seeing is one of the crack Federation squadrons."

"We came to the same conclusion," said the controller. "But their arrival here without being called is a bit too much of a coincidence."

As they watched the slow dance of lights on the screen a pattern emerged. The Rance group seemed to pull together, while the newcomers attempted to form an envelope around them. The

plot of lights on the screen gave very little hint of
the actual speeds and distances involved. Had the
maneuvering been visible to the naked eye, the
preparations for the coming battle would have
been an awe-inspiring sight.

Breathlessly the group in traffic control
watched the cluster of Rance ships try desperately
to avoid the closing trap. It was obvious, however,
that they were outclassed. They were being
driven into a tight nucleus while the attacking
force encircled them with an increasing semblance of symmetry.

Then the big blow came. For a moment the
screen went white as the receivers were over-
loaded with a burst of radiation that spanned right
into the radio frequencies. The attacking ships
alone were visible when the image straightened
and cleared. No significant ion traces were even
left to record the former presence of the disaster
ships. The destruction had been complete and
absolute.

Somebody in the room cheered. The reaction
spread to become a glorious sound of jubilation
and relief. The spaceport controller went to the
communications section, where his operators had
been attempting to make contact with the
liberators. Despite their efforts they still could
gain no reply. The mysterious fleet of ships
winked out one by one until the screen was as
empty as if no such fleet had ever existed.

"Commando action," said Ren. "No survivors
and no traces left. The Federation could deny
there had ever been a battle and nobody on Rance
could prove them wrong. We're the only witnesses and we're not likely to tell."

"So the Federation is awake to the merchant worlds' activities." San Weba had returned to Ren's side. "I always thought they must be. This isn't the first time I've heard of a Rance disaster fleet disappearing."

"Even so, we were lucky," said Ren. "Space is a big place. Even the Federation can't hope to police more than a very small fraction of it. The problem must be to know where the merchant worlds are going to move next. More than anything it's an exercise in good intelligence. It's tempting to hope that Federation intelligence spreads even to the Rim, but there's no sign on Roget of any Federation agency."

"Do you think this is the last we'll see of Rance?" asked Weba.

"The trade worlds must know they can't take on the Federation. If they suspect Federation influence here, they'll shy off like a shoal of startled fish. There are enough rich pickings in the galaxy that involve far less a risk. For myself I think Rance will forget the whole affair."

XVII

The sense of an unusual happening was strong upon Ren as he fetched the cushion-craft to a halt at the door of his chambers. A servant, obviously posted as a lookout, ran hastily to meet him as he waited for the air-cushion to subside.

"Master—the Lady T'Ampere has come to see you. She waits for you inside."

"To see me?" Ren was mildly surprised. It was evident, however, that his servant was more than a little impressed by the visit. In the activities of the past few weeks Ren had forgotten the mistress of Secondhill. The regulation of affairs in Anharitte had seemed so inextricably bound by the whims of the Lords Di Rode, Di Irons and Di Guaard—and the *Imaiz* himself—that there had seemed little room for feminine participation.

Intrigued, he made his way up the steps and turned into his chambers. The room seemed full of *Ahhn* servants paying attention to the one who sat regally awaiting his coming. Then, at a sign, all activity ceased and the room assumed an almost empty atmosphere as Ren approached.

"Lady T'Ampere?"

"Agent Ren, I take you to be."

"At your service, my Lady."

Ren looked at the wealth of colored veils, discerning beneath them the brightest, the most penetrating and the most dauntingly feline pair of eyes he had ever encountered. The veils were swept aside and the Lady T'Ampere rose to her feet and moved from the chair to meet him.

She was mature in years, yet by no means old. Her skin was far darker than was common among the *Ahhn* and was dry in texture, but strong character and something that had once been great beauty still shone from her countenance. She carried an aura—a presence—that stopped Ren in mid-stride and set him back on his heels. Here was one of nature's own aristocrats.

She motioned toward him.

"I would speak with you privately, Agent Ren." Her voice had the precise tone of one used to command. "Please have your servants leave us."

Ren turned and motioned to his staff to leave. He glanced at the Lady T'Ampere's retinue, expecting them also to be dismissed. When they stayed in their places he turned back to his visitor for explanation and was met by a mocking smile.

"The house servants of T'Ampere see much and hear much, but they never speak a word of what they learn. And do you know why, Agent Ren? It's because they have no tongues."

"No tongues?" For a moment he failed to grasp the implication of the phrase. When he did he was overcome with nausea.

"I can see by your face that you think me barbarous. But barbarity has to be assessed against a norm. For the house of T'Ampere my servants are the norm. Dion-daizan would kill me for this if he could—and that's why I'm here. I wish to offer you an alliance in your fight against Dion."

Forgetting to probe the etiquette of the situation, Ren sat down in the nearest chair, his mind still fighting the horror of the twenty or so deliberate mutes who surrounded their mistress. He was not at all sure he wanted to be joined in such a frightful allegiance.

"My feud with the Imaiz is a private affair," he said at last.

"Indeed? Is that why you tried to win the support of Di Irons, Di Guaard and Di Rode? Come, Agent Ren! I know my Anharitte and there's little you've said or done here that has not been relayed to me in detail. As you rightly surmised, Dion is playing with some very dangerous forces. If he succeeds the old way of life will fall. The flood will sweep away the aristocracy, the societies, the peace and stability of our times and certainly the free trade preference you yourself enjoy. What I think you misjudge is the violence of the flood."

Ren frowned. "Such situations are not beyond my experience."

"This one will be. Think of what would happen if my dumb cortege ever believed the old laws were ended. What nights of bloody horror would be precipitated?"

"To what nights of horror have your people already been exposed?" asked Ren coldly. "While I agree with you in principle, I abominate your practices."

"I'm not interested in your squeamish idealism. I'm talking about facts as they exist." Her curiously bright eyes fixed him with a gaze little short of hypnotic and her voice was like a band of steel. "Like it or not, you're committed to opposing Dion-daizan. Your lucrative free trade can't sur-

vive if he wins. Furthermore, in the blood bath
that will come if he's allowed to tip the scale too
far you'll pay equally with those who burn their
slaves or cut out their tongues. You're as much a
part of the old way of life as they. Make no mistake, Agent Ren—you're already one of the
damned."

"You have a proposition?" Ren asked at last.

"I have five hundred men at arms whom I'm
willing to place at your disposal for the storming
of Magda. I would expect you to use your influence with the societies to muster a similar force.
Not even Magda could stand for long against a
thousand men."

"It won't work," said Ren. "Di Irons would
never permit a pitched battle in Anharitte."

"Di Irons would be powerless against an army
of a thousand. What could he do—arrest them all?
But in any case, you may safely leave the prefect to
me. You would march under my banner—and a
noble house has right of arms anywhere in the city
at any time. I can assure you that on the day we
move the prefect and his men will be looking the
other way."

"I'll think it over," said Ren. "I'll need to sound
out the societies first."

"Then don't delay too long. Dion has a bill of
manumission set for consideration by the planetary government. Rumor has it that it'll be favor-
ably received. If it becomes law many slaves will
earn the right to become freemen—though their
sympathies will remain unchanged. At the moment we can move an army against Dion without
opposition. If the manumission bill goes through
the task will be much more difficult. A veritable
legion of freemen will be eager to delay us."

"I promise you an answer with all speed. Within a day I'll come to you on Secondhill and tell you what support we have. I think you'll have your way if I can sway the societies in that time."

"Then I'll look to receive you at this time tomorrow, Agent Ren. But let this warning spur you—if Dion wins don't hope for personal survival. Your support by and for the aristocracy is too well known for you to survive even a minor rebellion. If Dion's flood gates open you, too, will be flotsam on the tide."

The evening was a fine one. Breathing across the broad back of Firsthill, the warm winds from the sea gained a rich scent from the abundance of flowering trees and shrubs that flourished around the little squares and plazas. Here a trade cry and there a hint of music added texture to the air and endowed it with a sense of life.

The individually wrought and unplanned buildings, illuminated by the growing gold of evening, formed a picture that touched some unexpected vein of artistry in Ren's soul. He felt he wanted to impress the perfection of this image into some more permanent form, so that he could take it to some other time and relive this evening hour. Unfortunately he knew of no medium with the scope or fidelity to record the nuances of light, the scents and sounds and character of Anharitte. He could only promise himself that, whatever the outcome of his feud with Dion-daizan, the city as it now stood must never be destroyed.

The Lodge of the Pointed Tails was particularly impressive with its golden turrets and ornate red relief. Passing into its rich interior, Ren was once against lost in the lyric pictures that depicted the

bloody and glorious progress of the *Ahhn* out of
barbarism to their present proud community. The
message was not lost on him. The *Ahhn* civiliza-
tion was too newly acquired to have become an
innate precept. If it were disrupted at this stage,
every possibility existed that the whole society
would revert to the former pattern of savage warrior tribes and be set back five hundred years in
history.

In mid-stride Ren was caught by the realization
that in opposing Dion-daizan he had himself
adopted a measure of responsibility for the future
of the *Ahhn*. As representative of an outworld
power and in control of money and resources
comparable with those of the nobility, he was
equally responsible with Di Irons, Di Guaard and
the *Imaiz* for preserving the essential Anharitte.
No victory, however won, would taste anything
but bitter if the prize were destroyed in the winning.

As usual, Catuul Gras was expecting him. No
movement of persons of interest ever went unre-
ported to the scribe. Catuul had been practicing
shadow-fighting with some curiously old and ornate toothed swords when Ren entered. These
fearsome instruments he laid carefully on the
long table and addressed the weapons rather than
the agent.

"So the Lady T'Ampere has made her proposition?"

Ren felt his eyes drawn to the barbarous swords,
which were fashioned to inflict the most terrible
wounds in flesh, yet disengage cleanly—they
were weapons for use when no quarter would be
asked or given.

"She has. What do you know?"

"The house servants of Lady T'Ampere have no tongues. But whey can speak with their hands. And so can we. You acquitted yourself well in that conversation, friend Tito. She's one of the *abolii*."

The latter word was taken from the old *Ahhn* phrase for detestable. Ren had heard it used occasionally, but seldom with such feeling. He was gratified to note that the systematic mutilation of slaves was unpopular even with the societies.

– "The point is," said Ren, "do we accept her offer or not? I need your advice. And I need to know if the societies will cooperate."

"You ask two questions, friend Tito, and I give you two answers." Catuul took up one of the vicious swords and drove it savagely into the plaster of the wall. "My own advice to you is on no account become associated with T'Ampere in any way. The House of T'Empte made a similar mistake. Now T'Empte is an empty province. But nonetheless—the societies will find five hundred men. They don't favor the idea, but if Dion's bill of manumission is accepted by the planetary government, it will be the start of the end of us all. We must support even the *abolii* if we wish to preserve our way of life."

Ren took up the second sword and examined its toothed edge. Held closely, it lost its cumbersome appearance and the dreadful artistry of the razor teeth made him wince as he imagined its effect in battle. Its balance was perfect in his hands.

"The clans have already spoken then?"

"The elders have been holding council for days regarding Dion's bill. They have decided he must not be allowed to press the bill to law. To have five

hundred extra men from T'Ampere for the purpose is worth a pact with the devil."

"Then I may confirm to Lady T'Ampere that her
offer is acceptable?"

"Go at the agreed hour tomorrow. If there is any
change in the situation I'll contact you before you
go. If you don't hear from me, assume that it's safe
to accept T'Ampere's offer."

"Why so guarded?"

"Because the Lady T'Ampere had a visitor earlier today—before she came to you. Sonel Taw,
the castellan of Di Guaard. We don't yet know
what was said, but it's an absolute certainty that
my Lord Delph knew nothing of it. Mad he may
be, but even he would have no commerce with
T'Ampere. Tread very carefully, friend Tito.
There's great mischief in the making in Anharitte,
and T'Ampere is behind it."

XVIII

There was no castle on Secondhill. The once-great fortress of T'Ampere had been laid in ruins in some former conflict. Now its broken walls and chambers gaped amazedly at the sky, as if it could still not comprehend the fury that had destroyed it. At the foot of the ruins sat the neat circle of the chateau and the home estate. True, the complex was walled, but not in the sense of forming a stronghold in battle. T'Ampere's strength lay in other regions.

To reach T'Ampere, Ren had passed from Firsthill down through the slave market and crossed the ship lanes by slimboat. From here he had ascended Secondhill by the only access worthy of being called a road.

The way had wound steeply up between the great banks of a natural pass. During the climb he had seen no signs of life or habitation. Breaking suddenly over the brow of the hill he came upon the gates of the chateau before he had guessed their nearness. Unlike the other hills, each of which had an attendant township gathered outside the citadel, Secondhill contained only the walled seat of T'Ampere and immediately spread out to contain nothing but the broken, sheep-grazed slopes that reached down to the eastern plains and T'Ampere province.

Ren's first impression that the Chateau T'Ampere was undefended was soon corrected. His path toward the broad gates had placed him in a neat ambush. He found himself surrounded by some undoubtedly competent soldiery and was forcibly conducted to a barracks associated with the great house and there interrogated by an officer. When he had established his identity, a runner was despatched to ascertain Lady T'Ampere's wishes in the matter. The message came back that Ren would be summoned when the lady pleased. Fuming at the treatment he was receiving, Ren found himself locked in a cell for two hours until a guide came to conduct him to Lady T'Ampere.

The rooms of T'Ampere were depressing. Here was traditional *Ahhn* style used to an extreme extent, with carpets many centimeters thick strewn with cushions. Even the walls were smothered with heavy drapes and curtains. The screened windows admitted barely any light and what light did gain entrance was immediately absorbed by the browns and grays and blacks of the soft furnishings. Ren was reminded of the lair of a pampered cat—even the air seemed pungent with an overpowering feline smell. Here, he reasoned, was one more instance where nobility and absolute power over others had overfed itself to produce something mentally and physically unwholesome. It came to him that the *Ahhn* nobility had shown him little to commend its survival. Perhaps Dion's revolution was fated to succeed.

"You bring me an answer, Agent Ren?" T'Ampere rose from the gloom, bright-eyed like a jungle creature regarding its prey.

Ren longed to strike at the bright mockery. "Perhaps. But first I'd like an apology for being detained so long by your men. I came here at your invitation to answer a question you had asked. I resent being treated like a thief."

The amusement quickened in her face. "Believe me, if you saw what we did to thieves in T'Ampere, you would raise no such unjust accusation."

Ren saw she was playing with him and decided to deny her the pleasure of drawing a response. His dislike of the woman was now intense.

"Lady T'Ampere, yesterday you brought me a proposal—five hundred men at arms to use against Magda if the societies would provide a like number. This they've agreed to do."

"A firm decision so quickly?" The feline eyes narrowed. "Either you have remarkable powers of persuasion or the elders have become mortally afraid of Dion."

"They didn't take me into their confidence. In this matter I act only as messenger." Ren felt disinclined to elaborate.

"I doubt that's true." She shook her head impatiently. "But it's of no importance. At any rate we now have our alliance."

"We do not," said Ren abruptly. "I said the societies had agreed. I didn't say that I agreed."

A flicker of anger crossed her face. "And what objection do you have, merchant?"

"When I climbed Secondhill I had no objection. But I want now to know why I was detained. Was it to make me conscious I was not of the Anharitte nobility? Or was it to keep me out of the way while some other plans were entertained?"

"I find your impertinence less than amusing.

Do you suspect me of duplicity?"

"I suspect the alliance you offer is not as simple as you claim."

"Grief! And do you also have a name for these other activities in which you think I'm involved?" Her voice held steely contempt.

"At a guess I'd say they concerned Di Guaard and Sonel Taw."

Her face became clouded with disbelief then relaxed into laughter.

"You have my apology, Agent Ren. I mistook you for a fool. I see now why even Dion treats you with circumspection. You understand us far better than we understand ourselves. Let's stop fencing with each other and conclude our alliance. I perceive we make worthy partners in mistrust."

"When I need your men I'll send for them," said Ren. "I won't make advance plans with you, because T'Ampere has no talent for secrecy. When I ask for your men, you are to send the full five hundred without delay and they will respond to my lieutenants, not their own. Only on these terms can I afford to be involved with T'Ampere."

"You've been well schooled," she said thoughtfully. "It's a good sign. Very well, your terms are accepted. If you cover yourself as well against your enemies as you do against your allies, you should have a brilliant future in Anharitte. Indeed, I've a mind to make you a second proposition."

"Which is?"

"I could use a man of your caliber at T'Ampere. The rewards would be far better and above anything the Company could offer."

"In what capacity?" asked Ren without enthusiasm.

"Consort," said Lady T'Ampere.

Ren felt physically sick. "I'm afraid the proposition's unthinkable. For me to adapt to the ways of T'Ampere is not possible. For T'Ampere to adapt to me would need a major revolution."

"Then I'll order runners to light your way down the slopes. Such paths can be treacherous."

"In the high places of Anharitte all paths seem to be treacherous," said Ren.

Night had fallen by the time Ren left the Chateau T'Ampere. The beautiful Rim stars were spread in a wide, bright pattern and such was their illumination that torches were not actually necessary. Nevertheless a dozen runners with flares were waiting to guide him down the path toward Firsthill and the light from their brands at first obscured a shifting redness in the western sky.

Clear of the gates, Ren stopped and directed the runners to fall behind him so that he could better see the flame on the farther hill. An angry red patch seemed to burn on the left side of Firsthill, but its precise location was difficult to determine. As he continued down the pass the direct view of the conflagration was lost to him and its existence was told only by a continued redness in the sky.

At the river he bade the runners return to their mistress. A slimboat, attracted by the light of the flares, came to ferry him across the shipping lanes. The boatman had no knowledge of the fire on Firsthill, but opted for the direction of Di Guaard when questioned about its probable location. Having gained the shore, Ren hurried through the now deserted slave market and was soon in the complex streets at the top of the hill. A

trade call alerted him to the presence of a waiting
armsman from the Pointed Tails.

"Agent Ren, Catuul asked that I intercept you
on your return. He wishes to speak with you at the
lodge. We must proceed with caution."

"What's happening here?"

"The slaves of Di Guaard have set fire to the
castle. Rumor has it that Delph Di Guaard is slain.
The prefect and his men are now in attendance.
Catuul suggests it would be unwise for you to
enter the district."

"He's probably right. The timing of this affair is
not without significance. Lead me by a safe route
to the lodge."

The streets were crowded with sightseers drifting toward the scene of the fire. In the background
a shadowy traffic of hurrying men indicated the
messengers of various agencies going to report or
being sent again to keep up with the news. The
armsman hastened Ren through the slowly moving throng, turning aside always to avoid dark
places. A constant chatter of inquiry came from
opened upperstory windows as bewildered heads
tried to gauge the cause of the commotion. The
armsman stopped to engage no one in conversation. Though he did not speak of it, his movements seemed to anticipate danger at every corner
and his hands was forever hovering near his
sword.

Catuul Gras was waiting at the lodge.

"Is it true that the slaves of Di Guaard have
revolted?" Ren asked him.

Catuul nodded. "It's true. But they were incited
to revolt."

"By whom? Not the *Imaiz*, surely?"

"No, by the castellan, Sonel Taw. I think he saw in the ruse a chance to depose Lord Delph. But in any event he's failed."

"Were the prefect's men so quick to Delph's defense?"

"The prefect's men were unable even to pass the outer walls. By the time they reached the castle the fight was over and most of the slaves were contained. Which is fortunate, because if they had escaped into Anharitte and gained support from their fellows, the whole city would probably be afire by now."

"I sensed as much," said Ren. "Tensions are high in the streets tonight. But if Sonel Taw incited the slaves to riot, who was it who quelled them?"

"A hundred bondsmen from Magda," said Catuul, looking nowhere in particular.

"Magda? Slave against slave? To protect Di Guaard?"

Ren was fazed momentarily.

"I know you'd not believe me, friend Tito, but I can only speak what I know. Though I doubt if it was Delph Di Guaard's health they were interested in maintaining. I think they were as afraid as we of the incident's starting a general uprising. With seven slaves in the district for every freeman, tonight could have been one of the bloodier pages of history."

"And if Di Irons had been forced to call in the government forces, it would have been even bloodier." Ren nodded his acceptance of the logic. There was no doubt that if once the floodgates of violence were opened they would be extremely difficult to close.

A commotion at the door broke up the conversation. Three of the Pointed Tails armsmen were struggling to subdue a prisoner they had taken from the streets, who had broken away at the last moment. Fortunately they were men who knew their trade. Shortly a body was thrown through the door to land at Catuul's feet. The scribe turned the wretch over wonderingly, a short dagger held to the man's throat. With his windpipe in peril Sonel Taw, the castellan of Di Guaard, looked up from the floor in genuine anguish.

"Ah! The idiot is here," said Catuul with some satisfaction. "Witness the man who was crass enough to risk all Anharitte to satisfy his spite."

Sonel Taw noticed Ren and struggled to sit up. His face lit with an ingratiating smile of recognition.

"Agent Ren knows me. He'll tell you all is not as it seems. We have an understanding, the agent and I. Ren, keep these ruffians from my throat."

"I think not," said Ren. "What you've provoked tonight could well have killed us all. If you had a quarrel with Di Guaard, you should have tried it man to man. But to involve the slaves could have resulted in a massacre."

"But—" The castellan rose to his knees, his eyes searching piteously for comprehension. "But it was part of the plan—"

"What plan?"

"Hers—she told me of your intent—" Taw had the look of a man betrayed.

"That bitch T'Ampere," said Ren. "She's behind this. She thought by now to have me in her pocket."

"But you aren't?" inquired Catuul anxiously.

"I agreed to nothing more than to send for her men as and when I required them against Magda. Di Guaard wasn't even mentioned. In fact, she kept me at the chateau until Castle Di Guaard was well in flames."

"Good. Then we aren't compromised. Tonight's work has no reflection on our feud with the Imaiz. You're a man of good sense, friend Tito. And our fallen castellan here will find few to mourn his passing." Catuul bent forward again with the dagger.

Ren intervened.

"Send your men to deliver him to Di Irons. He's more the prefect's concern than he is ours. I think a few days at the hands of Di Irons' tormentors will be valuable to his education—and we've no time to lose over killing him."

"No time?" The Scribe regarded Ren curiously. "Your meaning escapes me."

"A hundred men from Magda came to Firsthill. A hundred of the same we'll have to fight if we storm the castle. Doesn't it make sense to see that as few as possible get back to Magda? They're on our territory and they've a river to cross. We have them at quite a disadvantage."

Catuul considered for a moment, then leaped to his feet, shouting orders and calling for men. His acceptance of Ren's point was immediate once he had explored the implications. He was secretly furious with himself for not having realized so vital a matter earlier. Much valuable time had been lost and the men from Magda must by now be dispersed through the city and be making their

way down to Firstwater. Leaving the hapless castellan in the company of armsmen charged with
the duty of delivering him to the prefect, Catuul
collected Ren and they sped out into the night.

XIX

A system of messengers and signals had alerted all the Pointed Tails, including those who acted as guards at the slave compounds on the edge of Firstwater. The first priority was to try to locate the boats the men from Magda would try to use for their return. The second was to locate and harass the enemy itself.

Ren found the whole operation confusing. Traveling at a steady run, usually by torchlight but occasionally by starlight alone, Catuul was a veritable mobile headquarters. Out of the darkness messengers would gather to exchange a few quiet words and be dispatched again to carry out some new command. Just how the messengers located Catuul Gras in the first place was quite beyond Ren's comprehension—the scribe was constantly on the move. But the system appeared to work and gradually some semblance of order grew in the middle of apparent chaos.

Resignedly Ren settled into a labored jog-trot, the nearest approach he could make to the *Ahhns'* effortless style of running. Nevertheless he found the going hard. At the foot of the Trade Road the scribe motioned the breathless agent to rest for a while.

"We're in luck, Friend Tito. The news is that

they've not yet crossed back over the water. Some were seen coming through the town and down the Blackslope. Others escaped down Sidepath and must be crossing the plain to join their fellows near the Black Rock. We've secured all the slim-boats along Firstwater, but it looks now as though they must have made the crossing farther west. Now we must drive along the riverbank as far as T'Empte Crossing and try to separate them from their boats.''

"Will we be in time?"

"Some are reported only a few minutes ahead of us and they may not yet realize we're after them. They've only to stop and wait for their comrades on the other route and we shall trap them."

Ren nodded. He felt the excitement of the chase and this piece of harassment would be an excellent chance to even the score with the Imaiz. He turned and followed Catuul eagerly toward the river.

The whole scene was so utterly devoid of sounds or people that he found it nearly impossible to believe that only a short distance ahead were a hundred men from Magda and a large attacking force of Pointed Tails determined to stop their escape into boats and across the river. After ten minutes Ren became seriously worried. He was almost within sight of T'Empte Crossing and along the bank the slimboats used by the ferrymen were neatly drawn to cover and undisturbed—but there still was no sign of Catuul or the enemy.

Then he stopped, rubbing his eyes with disbelief. At first he thought his vision tricked by the dim light, but the continuous shine across and above the surface of the water was no chimera—it persisted and was real. Yet the image seemed to have no connection with the circumstances in which he found it. Then, even as he watched, a sudden burst of flame on the far side of Secondwater reared upward and spread out along the curious shining thing spanning the river. The image began to collapse and Ren heard the shouts and calls of the Pointed Tails a little farther up the riverbank.

Passing Magda Crossing, where the slimboats were now well secured by grinning armsmen, they advanced along the bank of Secondwater. This part of the way was clearer, there being no wharves or buildings along the bank. Here open fields led to a line of trees at the water's edge and there was little concealment for men save the blanket of darkness. A series of trade calls began to sound from the direction of the Black Rock, now to their left across the fields, and Catuul answered them without hesitation.

"Magda's men are still on this side of the river," the scribe told Ren. "They gather near the old T'Empte Crossing about a kilometer hence. There'll be fighting—I'll leave you here. Make your way to the crossing carefully. I think our trap is sprung."

Catuul called his men around him and together they trotted ahead. Ren, whose occupation and outworld training had ill prepared him for such marathon running, regretfully watched them go. Although he was in excellent physical condition by outworld standards, he lacked schooling in the style that enabled the native *Ahhn* to continue running for hour upon hour with little sign of fatigue. He sat on a large projection of rock and rested for some minutes before continuing to walk slowly toward the appointed place.

Ren had thought to hear sounds of battle ahead, but all was silent. This made him wary—perhaps the men from Magda had avoided the contact and were even now moving back across the fields. The light from the stars was insufficient for him to see more than a short distance around him. Every tree had the capacity to be a potential point of ambush. He walked as near the river's edge as he dared, sword drawn and fully prepared to fight or run as the occasion might require.

Intrigued by this mystery, Ren hastened forward. He should, he thought, by now be able to hear the sound of steel on steel, or the slap of an *Ahhn* crossbow. Instead all he heard were voices and the unmistakable trade calls of the Pointed Tails carrying reports to those farther afield.

A rustling at the treeline made him stand, sword ready, until the call of a nightbird he recognized as Catuul's signature sounded close to him.

"The *Imaiz* has beaten us." Catuul Gras appeared suddenly at Ren's elbow. "Didn't I tell you he was a wizard?"

"What happened?" asked Ren. "Didn't you catch them?"

"They got away from us, all of them. Dion's magic made a bridge of mist across the river and they ran over it. We could have taken some of them, but none of us dared approach such a terrible thing."

"Damn! How did he manage that?"

"I know nothing of the ways of wizardry," said Catuul, slightly affronted.

"A rhetorical question. I was thinking out loud," said Ren. "Dion is no more a wizard then I am. And I tell you there's no such thing as a bridge of mist that can bear the weight of a man. There has to be some rational explanation."

Despite Catuul's obvious reluctance to follow, Ren moved along the river bank to where he had seen the curious shining thing on the water. Something submerged appeared to be distorting the surface of the river. He called for torches, but none were available.

"Mark this spot, Catuul, and guard it. At first light I want boats here to explore both banks and drag out anything in the water. The river here is best part of a hundred and fifty meters wide—and a thing that could carry a hundred men across it in a few minutes can't possibly have vanished without trace."

"Except a bridge of mist," said Catuul, still unconvinced.

Weary, Ren allowed himself to be escorted back to his chambers. Though his body was thoroughly tired, his mind persisted in wrestling with the problem of the intangible bridge. He could in no way reconcile a shine across the water and the scribe's description of a bridge of mist with anything capable of bearing the weight of a hundred men across the water yet able to vanish and leave no trace. Ren's education had prepared him with a good grounding in what physical parameters he could normally expect to encounter, but none of his knowledge of physics appeared relevant to the

case. He was unwilling to admit that some unknown scientific principle might be involved, yet
he was incapable of finding a satisfactory answer
by employing any known principles.

One reason for his intense preoccupation with
the problem was his projected scheme for the
storming of Castle Magda. He sensed in Catuul a
superstitious awe of the works of the Imaiz that
had to be dispelled if the campaign against Magda
were to be a success. Unless Ren could prove to
the Pointed Tails that the vanishing bridge was
only a clever trick, they would carry the attack
against Magda burdened with the fear of some
new manifestation of the Imaiz's magic. It was
easy to see that such a condition would give any
maneuver a rather precarious chance of success.

Firstlight seemed to come all too soon. Ren had
taken his problem to bed and had lain awake with
it for several hours despite his tiredness. When he
finally succumbed to sleep it was for a few hours
only. A servant came to wake him with the reminder that Catuul Gras would be waiting for him
at T'Empte Crossing. Cursing the scribe for his
apparent ability to do without sleep, Ren rose and
washed but refused the delay of breakfast.

Unable to face the long walk involved, he sent
for stavebearers and took the cushion-craft, fret-
ting all the way down the Trade Road amid the
morning traffic of carriers' carts. Once past the
Black Rock and free from the restrictive attentions
of the stavebearers, he turned off toward T'Empte
Crossing. For the last part of the journey he went
directly across the fields to where he could see a
group of Pointed Tails on the riverbank.

Catuul Gras received him with enthusiasm.

Several men were in the river, diving deep to recover volumes of some substance they hauled ashore in a continuous strand and piled for Ren's inspection. Boats from the farther shore were fetching back a curious item found abandoned on the sandy beach, the purpose of which was completely obscure to the native *Ahhn*.

When the collection was complete, Ren inspected it briefly and the concept immediately fell into place. The shine across the waters, the idea of a bridge of mists, the carrying of a hundred men across the river—all these puzzles suddenly had an explanation. Ren swore mightily when he realized the nature of the objects before him. Behind his comprehension was an absolute certainty that the *Imaiz* was nothing more than a clever technician with a typically Terran training.

The items with which he had been presented consisted of a continuous length of heavy-gauge polythene sheet formed into a tube of a diameter more than sufficient to admit a standing man, and a primitive large-capacity air bellows. Some sort of rush matting had additionally been provided to spread the weight of a man traversing the interior of the tube over water. A quantity of rope had been recovered which presumably had been used to haul the flexible "tunnel" across the river and to secure it in place.

"Tell me how it works," implored Catuul Gras.

Ren pursed his lips. "It's an old Terran device. That large plastic tube, when filled with air, will float and will easily bear the weight of a man on the water. Fitted with flaps through which a man can enter without losing too much air and an air pump sufficient to keep it filled, it makes a floating bridge. It's cheap, simple, and expendable— you can afford to set fire to it if you fear your enemies might try to follow you across."

"Then it isn't magic?" asked Catuul. He sounded almost disappointed.

"Far from it. In a smaller and modified form it's used in a common Terran water sport—men tie themselves into large plastic bubbles and run races over lakes and rivers. It's simply the clever application of a common outworld principle."

"Which reinforces your suggestion that the Imaiz is a Terran?"

"I don't know." Ren thought about his answer carefully. His words were colored by a new caution. "There's a Terran influence, certainly—but that could be acquired from books. The main factor that emerges from this affair is that Dion and his men are effectively policing Anharitte. They seem to be trying to prevent a castastrophic breakdown of your society even as they are undermining it. A restructuring without a revolution. Quite a trick—if you can achieve it."

"But didn't Dion break faith with his own at Di Guaard yesterday? Slave against slave was something no one had expected."

"He broke faith only if you assume that his interest is the emancipation of the slaves. But perhaps his real policy is a larger purpose—that of emancipating the Ahhn as a race. But in any event I can't see that either free trade or the societies can survive the transition. We're both part of the old pattern."

"So you intend to go through with your march on Magda?" asked Catuul gravely.

"To Magda it is. And in view of Dion's man-umission bill this may well be the last chance we'll get. I propose we strike Magda as soon as possible and with the largest force we can muster. Whatever happens, we musn't fail. A great many people will be watching the battle. If we lose, the Imaiz will not only gain Anharitte but probably his policies will win him all Roget as well. Our assault on Magda could have a great bearing on the shape of history. That's why we must plan it well."

"What did you mean by the emancipation of the Ahhn?" asked Catuul after a while.

"It's a relative concept that would only be ap-parent if you'd lived outworld," said Ren, realiz-ing his mistake.

XX

At the head of the Trade Road the watchmen were waiting for Ren to return. Their interception of him was swift and deliberate. The stavebearers were halted.

"What's the meaning of this?"

"The prefect requires your presence, Agent Ren."

"Again? This is becoming too much of a habit. But it's early and I've not yet breakfasted. Tell him I will come to him later."

The leading watchman shook his head. "Our orders were to bring you in all haste. The Lord Di Irons is in a fury."

"Then I'm afraid his fury must wait for a proper time. Stand aside."

Ren had observed that the stavebearers had drawn to the side of the road and the way in front of him was clear save for the three watchmen. The craft's cushions were still inflated and he doubted the law-enforcers would stand in the path of the vehicle if it began to move. He edged it forward, slowly at first to warn the men out of his way, then faster. He was gratified to note that they made no attempt to halt his progress, but retired to the road's edge to discuss the situation.

Ren continued swiftly, having no thought of returning for the stavebearers who still stood waiting for a decision from the watchmen. When he was out of weapon range, he began to breathe more freely. This had been a trial of strength between himself and the authority of D Irons—and for the moment he had won. As he drove unescorted to the fruit market he honestly questioned his own motives for refusing to accede to the watchmen's demands. He found his reasons not as clear as they had seemed moments earlier. As one of the prime movers of events in Anharitte, he had come to resent the prefect's imperious demands on his time. Yet now he thought about it, it grew more plain that he was attempting to set himself up above the law—and the only persons above the law in Anharitte were the lords.

He became interested—and slightly apprehensive—about how Di Irons would react. At worst, and if it suited the prefect's purpose, Di Irons would be justified in detaining him and demanding his deportation. At best, Di Irons might overlook the slight and await Ren's coming at a later hour. Ren's surmises, however, in no way covered the actual reaction his stand had provoked.

Within the hour Di Irons himself was announced on his doorstep.

"Didn't you hear, Tito, that I needed words with you at once?"

"My apologies, Prefect, but I was about early and was greatly in need of food. I was coming to see you soon."

The prefect waved the matter aside impatiently and accepted a place at Ren's table.

"First I have to thank you for sending me Sonel Taw. Under threat of torement he has told me much that explains last night."

"Did he kill Di Guaard?" asked Ren.

"The fool tried, though I doubt if he had the courage to perform the deed himself. Di Guaard died in the fire, nonetheless. But that isn't why I wanted words with you. Taw also hinted at a liaison between you and the Lady T'Ampere. Can this be true?"

"Liaison's too strong a term. She has offered me men to reinforce my society in feud against Dion-daizan."

"At what price?"

"I struck no bargain on price. She claims Dion is out to kill her—which may or may not be true, though I hope it is—and she offered me help if I would lead a strike against him. This I've agreed to do, but on my own terms."

"How many men did she offer?" Di Irons seemed angry, not with Ren directly but seemingly with all the world.

"She suggested five hundred—if the society would find a like quantity."

"Five hundred? T'Ampere has five thousand to use if she chooses. If you should take Magda, what do you suppose will happen to the rest of Magda province?"

"I'd not given the matter a thought."

"Then I'll tell you. With the Imaiz removed, T'Ampere would take the rest of the province, because nobody, not even I, could stop her. You're the only man in Anharitte who would dare to take arms against Dion-daizan, so she sees you in a useful catspaw. If you should succeed, you will hand her Magda province on a plate. If you lose she's lost at most five hundred men. Do you now see in what you've become involved?"

"I hadn't known the details of her ambitions," said Ren. "Therefore I find your warning timely. But I'm not sure it modifies my plan."

"I hadn't expected you to be easily swayed. But if you're still intent on turning Thirdhill into a battle ground, you should at least know in what cause your blood is being spilled. It's your life balanced against her gain. Do you think it a fair bargain?"

"Are you trying to warn me not to proceed with the exploit?"

"I don't give a damn whether you proceed or not. You've almost no chance of winning and a very high chance of getting killed in the attempt. Even if you win, T'Ampere will take the major prize. You can work out the odds for yourself. But I warn you—you're engaged in an unholy alliance if you've listened to T'Ampere. She's made the almost identical proposition to most of the lords in the past, but history has taught them caution. Only T'Empte ever fell for the ruse."

"Catuul Gras spoke of T'Empte as an empty province. What happened to the House of T'Empte?"

"The House of T'Empte was destroyed partly by T'Ampere's treachery and partly because Dion's revenge was so terrible. Since T'Empte was the catspaw, T'Ampere escaped more lightly. The old vixen's been sitting nursing her wounds these many years, waiting for someone else for her to thrust first into the fight with Dion."

"And now you think I've been elected?"

"You're the first new major force to emerge in Anharitte since the destruction of T'Empte. It was only a matter of time before you became included in her schemes."

"I'll mark well what you've said," said Ren. "I promise it will be taken into account before a decision is reached. But if I decide to storm Magda—where will I find my Lord Di Irons standing?"

"Slightly to your rear, looking the other way. You're taking T'Ampere's banner. Noble house against noble house still has legitimacy—they have the right to bear arms anywhere in the city. Even the planetary government couldn't object to your action under T'Ampere's shield. But the cost of digging your graves will certainly be passed on to your Company."

"You paint a black picture."

"Traditionally the rocks of Thirdhill have been awash with the blood of attackers since the stones of Castle Magda were first raised. I see no reason to suppose that this occasion will be any different."

Slowly Ren's plans took shape. Dubious at first, Catuul Gras rapidly became an enthusiastic convert when he saw the scope of thoroughness of the agent's ideas. Much preliminary work needed to be done and Catuul's standing with the elders of the clans foreshortened many otherwise lengthy negotiations. A large quantity of small boats was purchased along the coast to provide ready transport both for the attack and the unlikely event of a forced withdrawal. Canvassing around the Tyrene villages produces scores of useful contacts whose services would be needed when the great day came. Ren watched the steadily mounting bill for purchases and bribes and knew that this was going to be his final attempt. If this venture failed, he was unlikely to be given the money or the opportunity to try again. He had to succeed.

The more involved Catuul Gras became with the planning of the exploit, the more he began to appreciate how Ren's unique outworlder's view of Anharitte threw up ideas and perspectives by no means apparent to those who had spent their lives in the city. Although Ren's knowledge of *Ahhn* history was not complete, his understanding of the causes and motivations of political events was a revelation to the scribe. Ideas which in outline were received in doubtful silence won enthusiastic favor when Ren placed them in careful context. Whatever the results of the coming battle, the event was certain to find a permanent place in Anharitte's history.

For Ren the affair was necessarily a compromise. After his experiences with Alek Hardun he felt compelled to eschew the benefits of modern outworld weaponry. This limited his armory to what could be made or found from native resources. However, he felt no such limitations on his ingenuity. Many *Ahhn* craftsmen found themselves building instruments of siege and war which belonged not to their own history but to that of another race far across the legendary stars.

Logic dictated that rocket projectiles would have been more effective against Magda than ballistae and chain-cannon, but Ren was aware of a growing sense of responsibility toward the *Ahhn*. The release of too much advanced weaponry into their feudal society could have destroyed them just as effectively as if the ships of Rance had succeeded in their task. Alternately to go into battle ill-prepared was to invite disaster.

Nor were the words of Di Irons on T'Ampere overlooked. In his planning Ren had attempted to cover all of the many aspects of the exercise brought to his attention and several facets which he had determined for himself. Overall he had contrived to construct a time of chaos such that even the prefect would find it difficult to determine exactly what was taking place. It was also hoped that even the *Imaiz's* spies would present such a mass of irrelevant information to Dion that much could be achieved before the true pattern of the attack became apparent. All in all, Ren was rather pleased with his design. He was certain that Director Vestevaal would have given the whole scheme his heartiest approval.

At last Ren was ready to make his move. With the initial attack on Magda scheduled for late afternoon a messenger was sent that morning to call out T'Ampere's men. The messenger returned with the news that the party from Secondhill would join them at midday. This was largely as Ren had anticipated. He then waited for reports from the spies he had posted on T'Ampere's borders before ordering his men into the field.

His judgment proved correct. Coincident with the sending of five hundred men from T'Ampere to join Ren's sortie against Magda, the mistress of Secondhill had ordered nearly ten times that number of men to the shores of the River Daizan in the east, flanking Magda province. When he had received confirmation of this fact, Ren caused signals to be flown to set in motion the next phase of his plan. T'Ampere was due for a nasty shock.

The notion pleased Ren—it was with a wolfish smile on his face that he went to marshal his own forces. Against agreement, the five hundred from T'Ampere came complete with their own officers. These were neatly disarmed by the Pointed Tails and removed from the scene with some alacrity. Moreover, the five hundred were outnumbered at least two to one by members of the Pointed Tails and other societies brought in by Catuul as reinforcements. Lacking more direct orders from T'Ampere, the five hundred accepted the viewpoint offered them and soon became integ   in the total army marching on Thirdhill.

It was thus with fifteen hundred men rather than a thousand that Ren crossed Firstwater to Magda's shores. Here again his strategy was not immediately obvious. Instead of taking the hill road leading directly up to the township and thence to the castle, his men marched round at the foot of the slopes defining the hill—only when they had formed a full circle around Thirdhill did they begin to ascend. Even then their activity was limited. At the rough contour where the grasslands gave way to the steeper outcrops of gray rock on which the township and castle of Magda stood, they halted and began to prepare their positions as if in readiness for a siege rather than a direct attack.

Below the siege line other teams were busy setting up the various engines and devices of Ren's design and dragging them up the hill to stations at carefully determined points. The sun set on a deceptively quiet scene, the growing glow of campfires spreading out along the side of the hill like a string of bright beads. In only a few places did activity continue after nightfall.

Watchers in Castle Magda could have seen little of
these secret details, because the devices were still
concealed in dead ground and safely out of sight
of the castle.

The first sign of renewed action came when the
fires on the hillside facing Firstwater leaped into
new life as blocks of pitch and barrels of crude tar
were thrown upon them. The lazy breeze from the
southwest carried the heavy smoke in the direction of the castle and effectively screened the
movements Ren had planned for his secret weapons. These he now deployed forward to occupy
positions behind preselected outcrops of rock that
would serve to shield them from direct fire. Having relocated the devices to his satisfaction, Ren
returned to a safe position to await the coming of
first light.

Dawn brought the first skirmish. The defenders of Magda, apparently reluctant until now to
show their awareness of the army gathered
around them, sent out a reconnaissance party to
test the strength of the enemy. The Pointed Tails
were ready for them. Although Dion-daizan's
men bore small muskets of a type similar to those
favored by the ill-fated Di Guaard, they were no
match for the hail of steel shafts from the
crossbows of the society armsmen. The reconnaissance party lost two men and retreated
quickly back inside the castle gates. The attackers
lost no men at all in the incident and achieved a
great improvement in morale.

The coming of the early sun brought a slight
freshening of the wind, which nevertheless held
its prevailing course. This was precisely what Ren
had hoped and led naturally into the next phase of

his campaign. With the majority of his troops still holding a tight ring around the outer slopes, he again caused certain fires to be made to smoke and, under cover of the dense vapor clouds, he and twenty selected men gained the forward positions where their secret weapons had been sited. The fires were doused at a signal and into the clearing air above the frowning castle a large balloon rose uncertainly, trailing a canister on a rope beneath it.

This first balloon rose too slowly and snagged against a high battlement, its canister dangling against the outer wall. After a time the burning fuse expired and the canister fell outside the wall to explode at its foot. Although the explosive was a native product, its quality was sufficient to make a very credible bang. In its situation it did not damage, but it was a welcome foretaste of what such a device could do if it fell inside the castle confines.

The next balloon was prepared in recognition of the fate of the first. It rose more swiftly, clearing the battlements with ample margin. The fuse, too, had been altered and made slightly longer and the attackers had the immense satisfaction of seeing the canister plummet from a height and fall squarely inside the castle walls. There was no way to assess what damage the explosion might have caused, but its arrival must certainly have been a trial to the defenders. Much structural damage was not to be expected, but the more sophisticated the defenses, the more they would suffer from casual bombardment.

Eight more balloons were released. The first six

all delivered their explosive charges somewhere within the castle confines. Although they were subjected to rapid musket fire from inside Magda, the small balls projected by the weaponry were insufficient to damage the balloon fabric in any way that appreciably foreshortened the flight. The seventh balloon was shot down well before it had covered the distance to the castle. Ren fancied that a more powerful weapon, such as a Terran rifle, had been brought to bear on this. The eighth balloon was shot to pieces almost immediately upon release, and Ren and his comrades scarcely escaped with their lives as the canister fell back on top of them.

Seeing the growing effectiveness of the defensive measures, Ren decided that the idea had been taken far enough. Under cover of a new wave of smoke he ordered a retreat and made his way back to his now jubilant forces, quite satisfied with the progress he had made. Seven explosive charges had been delivered into Magda and although they would not have caused very much damage to such a massive structure, their effect both physical and psychological on the defenders could not have been negligible. Most gratifyingly, all this had been accomplished without the loss of a single man.

Meanwhile, Catuul Gras had been visiting the township below the castle. He had found the people fully aware of the situation and anxious about their own lives and property. Catuul had struck a bargain with them—he would restrict armed offensives to the vicinity of the castle proper if the townsfolk would agree to attempt no action in support of Dion-daizan. His proposal had been rejected until he pointed out the strength of the attacking force and the indefensibility of the scattered conglomeration of buildings of the township. If defied, he had said, he was quite prepared to raze the town by fire. On this point of understanding he had taken his leave, but had not forgotten to post pickets on all paths out of town as a reminder to the townsfolk that they were not free agents in this time of war.

Ren was concentrating now on moving his men up closer to the castle, so that he could start to use the engines he had brought. The maneuver proved more dangerous than he had calculated. The muskets of Magda proved to have an unexpected range and accuracy—and at least one high-powered rifle, probably with telescopic sights, was being deployed against his men. His losses were mounting, despite all his efforts at caution, and it became obvious that a daylight attack would be suicidal. Reluctantly he retreated to the safety of the siege line and caused his ballistae to be prepared.

He had intended the ballistae to be used at shorter range, but he knew that the smaller missiles could be hurled for considerable distances, though the accuracy of range left much to be desired. Fortunately, knowing of the strength of Magda's walls, he had not intended to try to use brute force to make a breach. Instead he had concentrated primarily on the manufacture of fire bombs. These were earthenware vessels filled with inflammable spirit and ignited by a wick, which would burst and spread a formidable area of flame around the point of impact.

Now Ren rearranged the ballistae for maximum effect at a distance and had the smaller fire bombs segregated ready for loading. The losses his force had sustained earlier in the day weighed heavily on his conscience. With this in mind, he was overcautious about keeping his men well under cover and out of the line of fire. Here he sensed he was failing in his duties as a commander of an aggressive force. He grudgingly acknowledged that he was a merchant concerned with profit and loss rather than life and death and that he placed more faith in the unorthodoxy of his weapons to gain Magda than he did in the power of flesh and bone to storm a castle so well defended.

The ballistae functioned well. About sixty per cent of the projectiles actually fell within the walls of Magda. The effect was difficult to gauge, but the persistence of smoke trails long after the spirit would have naturally burned out was evidence that at least some of the fire bombs had ignited combustibles within the castle. He had a mental picture of the vessels smashing against walls and windows and the torrents of flaming spirit being spattered well into the interior of Magda's installations. Apart from a direct hit, it was doubtful whether the practice would do much damage to the personnel, but no organization, however structured, could function without stress in the face of rapid and randomly occurring outbreaks of fire.

XXI

While he was engaged in pressing this newest mode of attack Ren had a visitor. Di Irons, grim and heavy and rustily bearded, pulled himself up the slopes and was guided to the place where Ren was directing operations. The prefect gave the impression of being tired of his world.

"If ever a man could name a common cause for all his misfortunes that man is I. And the name of the misfortune is Tito Ren. What are you trying to do, Tito? Set all Anharitte on fire?"

"Only Castle Magda—at the moment. Did you have something on your mind, Prefect?"

"The Tyrene attacked again—the first time in over forty years. It's too much of a coincidence to suspect your hand isn't behind it. Only a historian could have planned a coup like that. Don't you agree?"

Ren shrugged blandly. "They always told me the Tyrene pirates were a myth. I may be blamed for interfering with your history, but it seems to be taking the point a bit far to include mythology. Perhaps the ghost of Di Guaard has chased them from the cellars of the dead?"

"I'll wager it was some more lively spirit," said Di Irons heavily. "Especially as you canvassed heavily along that shore."

"Tell me about their coming," asked Ren innocently.

"T'Ampere lost a fortune. To protect the chateau itself she had to call back much of the army she had originally sent to the edge of Magda province. They were so late returning that the chateau itself had been overrun in the meantime. The Tryene took every single thing of value including her considerable treasury, fired the chateau, then retreated to the river. T'Ampere's men tried to give chase but were balked by the fact that you had already acquired all the available boats. To complete her misfortune Dion's men followed those she had called back and have occupied several of T'Ampere's own estates."

"Aiee!" shrieked Ren. "And I thought all the action was taking place up here."

"Far from it. And I'd advise you not to get too close to T'Ampere in the future. She knows well whom to blame for today's work. Clever you may be, but your ways are rather obvious."

"Did you climb all this way just to offer me that advice?"

"Not really. I was interested in your progress against Dion. You realize, of course, that your continued presence here is not due to your own efforts, but due to some reluctance on the part of Dion to swipe you away as one would a fly."

"I doubt the truth of that, but I'd be interested in knowing how you come to that conclusion."

"It's a factor most of us tend to forget, but one brought well to mind by Dion's occupation of some of T'Ampere's estates today. To us, soldiers are all freemen, mercenaries or armsmen of societies. But even slaves will fight in the service of Dion-daizan—and today a great many of them fought against T'Ampere. Furthermore, they were both armed and trained. Consider the implication, Tito. Dion can outman your army ten to one any time he chooses and not even feel the strain. And the majority of his men are already outside Castle Magda—they have you surrounded."

"There's been no sign of interference from his men in the province."

"Then the fact that he hasn't called on them must mean either that he considers you no threat or that he's confident that his garrison here can deal with you adequately on their own. Your prospects don't look too bright either way."

Ren surveyed the sky. The sun was already beginning to draw down on the horizon.

"Did you ever think, my Lord, that the Imaiz may not be infallible? When darkness falls I intend to take these ballistae closer so that we can throw even larger jars of flaming spirit inside those walls. No matter how good his defenses, they can't function if they're afire. When the garrison is fully occupied putting out blazes, we'll launch our main attack on the gates. If we can manage to breach even one gate successfully we'll run whole barrels of spirit inside the walls and fire these also. We have the catapults, we have the ramps and we have more than enough combustibles to fill Magda with a sea of flame. Are you thinking that Dion can withstand even that?"

"It's a good plan and a bold one," said Di Irons grudgingly. "On the face of it, you should succeed. But I'll wager the Imaiz knows every detail of the scheme. If he has not yet moved against you, it's because he knows your chances of success are quite remote."

"On that point we'll agree to differ. Only the

morning will tell which of us was right."

"I think you'll find it a long night. And I wish you welcome to it, Tito. This is one night I've no wish to spend on Thirdhill. If I can't persuade you to your senses, I'll take my leave. I think tomorrow there'll be many graves to supervise."

When the prefect had gone, Ren spared no time in calling together his lieutenants and ensuring that they were all in accord with the details for the coming battle. The ballistae were handed over to teams which had been instructed carefully on both the method and the timing of their use. The general relocation of troops had already begun and every foreseen aspect of the campaign had been fully covered. After a final inspection of the stockpiles of inflammables and the supply lines on which so much of the plan depended, Ren gave the final order to proceed.

Though no one knew it but himself, he had approached his final moment of decision with mixed feelings. Di Irons was a hard-headed realist, whose knowledge of probabilities in Anharitte was not to be dismissed lightly. Di Irons had predicted that the attack would fail. While Ren did not concur, he had to allow that the prefect's opinion was based on lifelong experience in Anharitte and carried a great deal of weight. Ren was not one to dismiss informed opinion lightly, and to underestimate Dion-daizan could be fatal.

Because he and Catuul were to join the selected armsmen who were to make the attack on the main gates, Ren and the scribe made a circuitous journey first west and then north to a point well

below the township, where part of the attacking
party was mustering. Here were men fresh into
the field, having just arrived up the Magda Road
where they had been encamped as a reserve. They
had completed their journey on time and Catuul
was pleased to find that everything was in excellent order.

The close warmth of the early night was beginning to fade as the assembled troop moved off up
the ragged road that followed the upward slope
between the dark ridges of the hill. The prognosis
for the attack was promising. Ren had handpicked
men fresh to the battle and backed them up with
small carts carefully laden with more than sufficient inflammables to fire the castle. Even Catuul
was beginning to feel that the operation must
succeed.

The wheels of the carriers' carts which regularly used this route had worn shallow grooves
into the granite of the underlying rocks. In the
moonless light from the Rim sky Ren found these
furrows a useful guide, presenting a surface certainly more congenial to walk upon than the broken roughness of the rest of the road. About fifty
men were ahead of him and as many following. In
the true tradition of the societies the whole column moved silently, neither singing nor talking,
their soft steps giving no indication that an army
was on the march. Even the wheels of the little
carts had been muffled. Ren found their quietness
almost eerie. He was acutely conscious of the
sound of his own boots on the hard underfooting.

The catastrophe was all the more terrifying because it lacked any warning. Many of those who

died scarcely had time to raise a shocked scream to their lips before they were destroyed. From somewhere out of the darkness a giant boulder, roughly spherical, plunged from a high place and thundered with sickening momentum between the cheeks of the road. Such was its force and unexpectedness that the first part of the column was crushed before the men had time to realize the nature of the thing which had leaped upon them. Comprehension of the nature of the threat was accompanied by a wild scramble by those following to climb the banks to avoid being mashed.

Weighing many hundred tons, the boulder had been finely calculated to fit the contours of the road without becoming embedded in the banks. Its trajectory must have been set for maximum effect in this precise application. Certainly its release from a place of rest on an adjacent hillside was no accident, but even the authors of the misfortune could scarcely have hoped for such a truly devastating effect. The boulder went straight through the column of marching men, grinding flesh and bone alike into the dust. Even the frail carts at the rear were crushed completely, together with the patient animals and the men who held their reins. The only ones who were spared were those who were quick enough to break formation and climb the bank in time to save themselves.

Aghast, Ren rose from the side of the bank where he had thrown himself and tried to estimate the severity of the damage. At least thirty were dead and as many more injured. The enormity of the damage and its improbable swiftness robbed him of words. The impact of that one great stone somehow symbolized all he had been told of the wrath of the Imaiz. In abstract such anger had been something to face with equanimity—translated into crushed flesh and shattered bones, its aspect assumed a far more daunting hue. The rumble of the boulder still traveling down the distant slopes was audible above the cries of the injured. Ren was sick on the spot.

Catuul Gras had taken command while Ren attempted to draw himself out of his shock. Already messengers had been sent to fetch help and sick-wagons for the injured. The fit men had been drawn aside and counted and lost weapons were replaced by arms taken from the dead. In the battle the Pointed Tails remained practical to the last.

"Friend Tito, we're ready to proceed."

The scribe was sympathetic toward Ren's condition, but knew the whole battle was lost if the commander faltered. Ren, feeling the true pains of responsibility for the massacre of so many of those he had hired, would have preferred to have retired from the fight at that point. It had once more been driven home to him that he was a merchant, not a soldier, and that fighting was only a part of a commander's burden—the other part was the acceptance of death, his own and those of his men. This was one aspect of making war that had never been apparent to him in books.

At the back of his mind the clear voice of conscience reminded him that those who had died had given their lives for the maintenance of the free trade principle—but the benefits of the prin-

ciple's survival would go almost entirely to the
nameless outworld moguls who controlled the
strings of interstellar trade. Catuul's men had died
in the service of someone else's greed.

XXII

Ren pulled himself together suddenly. The realities of the situation became brutally clear. Whatever the morality, he was already committed. There could be no turning back.

"I'm with you, Catuul. Have you sent for reinforcements?"

"No. But we'll be joining the rest of the party at the township. That'll have to be enough. They'll have extra combustibles also."

The remaining element of the troop continued with the march. Heeding the lesson so desperately learned, they broke file and walked high on the banks above the road in case a second boulder should follow the first. To their right the hill rose steeply into the blackness of a coniferous wood perched precariously high against the towering skyline and it was a reasonable certainty that those responsible for launching the boulder were still up there among the trees.

Catuul called for scouts and sent them ahead up the bank to ascertain what dangers might still be lurking. Ten minutes later a minor landslide heralded something rolling down the slopes. Cautious investigation revealed the bodies of the scouts with their throats cut. They had been rolled back down to rejoin their comrades. At no time had there been any sight of or sound from the hidden enemy, and Catuul viewed the road ahead with considerable apprehension.

Ren decided on a detour. His reasoning was that their progress along this particular road had been anticipated and the route would probably contain several further traps. If they struck a new path across country, they might encounter nothing more than random patrols. Catuul agreed and the party made a wide detour that much later fetched it to the road at the entrance to the township.

Here the rest of the attackers were waiting—and listening to an agitated messenger who had been unable to locate Catuul in the darkness. The messenger held a long and involved conversation with Catuul and repeatedly pointed beyond Magda to where Ren was beginning to discern a broad area of light in the sky. Finally Catuul approached him to report.

"Some of the ballistae are in trouble. Dion used cannon to knock a couple of them out. He had also managed to project some sort of incendiary into two of our stockpiles. The fires you see are our own emplacements burning."

"Have we still enough ballistae to set Magda afire?"

"Easily enough. We've seven left and even three would be adequate."

"Then let them commence firing. The quicker we can move now, the more surely we can win. Are we ready to assault the castle gates?"

"The men are ready. We're waiting for some more tar and oil to get through to replace some we lost, but it can follow us later. First we have to get into attack position."

"Then let's get on with it," said Ren. "We've still a fair way to go to reach the castle and Dion's obviously expecting us."

Soon the sounds of renewed hostilities became loud in the air. The night sky began to echo to the firing of muskets and the occasional roar of cannon. Although nothing was yet to be seen, Ren knew that his ballistae must have already started launching the great spirit jars over Magda's walls. Soon he hoped to see evidence of fires within the castle perched directly above where he now stood. It was necessary that his assault troops moved swiftly into position ready to seize the most advantageous time to breach the gates. Ren began to feel better. His previous horror was soon lost in the preoccupation of renewed activity.

The township of Magda was built of streets steeply sloped toward the castle at its head. The inhabitants had wisely stayed inside their houses and behind locked doors—the streets were deserted save for where Ren's army thronged the lower square. The way ahead up the narrow cobbled street was lit by occasional watch flares which dimly illuminated the way almost to the foot of the castle.

Despite the apparent overtness of the action Catuul insisted that a small troop of men go ahead to ensure that no ambush had been laid from the dark alleys that laced the township. Ren felt that his role should have placed him at their head, but he acquiesced to Catuul's more informed objection. Catuul needed men he had trained. The scouting party would be visible right to the top of the hill and could easily exchange signals with the men below.

Ren's decision to remain was nearly the cause
of his immediate death. The square was flanked
by buildings formed from the traditional granite
of the hills. Without warning—and by obvious
design—one of these collapsed, its walls falling
outward to scatter granite blocks far across the
square and on the heads of the unfortunate troops
mustered beneath. The nature of the mechanics
by which this trick was wrought was not apparent, but its effect was catastrophic. As the walls
had begun to bulge Catuul had thrown Ren clear
and the agent had received merely a startled impression of an apparently solid wall of masonry
seeming to become plastic as it bent and twisted
outward to engulf a great many of his men.

Shaken by his second near escape of the evening, Ren's reaction this time was one of immense
anger. He was sure the scheme could not have
been devised and executed without the foreknowledge and cooperation of the inhibitants and
he charged Catuul to make them pay for their
indiscretion as soon as it was light. Meanwhile
Ren's own task was becoming increasingly urgent. The scouting party reported by light signals
that the way was apparently safe and clear. Leaving fresh dead and wounded to be extricated from
the ruins of the building, Ren started up the road,
calling for men to follow him to the gates of
Magda.

Had he given the matter more thought Ren
might have been less brave. As he strode ahead he
realized that even in the dim flarelight his merchant's costume must have made him conspicu-
ous among the armsmen and rendered him an
easy target for a trained sniper. A sharpshooter

with a modern electron-optic rifle hidden in one of Magda's towers could have killed him at any moment. From his experience with the balloons Ren was reasonably certain that Dion did possess some of these weapons. He was forced to recognize that he was relying on the *Imaiz* voluntarily limiting his show of arms to those that would seem to be appropriate to the type of battle being offered.

Both he and Dion were playing a game—a war game carefully dressed to suit the character and background of Anharitte. But at what point would Dion's hand be forced so that he would be playing a game no longer? At some point before he was broken, the *Imaiz* would be forced by the dictates of survival to drop the pretense and reply with whatever weapons he possessed, regardless of their origin or propriety. Or did Dion truly have his boulder and falling-wall technique so well organized that even now he had no fear of the army moving up the sloping street?

Halfway up the hill Ren heard a shout from the men above him. He called back, anxious to know what they had found. He was not long left doubting. With a hideous clatter a large wheeled cart, heavily laden with blocks of stone and held unnoticed in some recess, had begun to run down the slope toward him. The very narrowness of the street precluded the escape of all but the lucky as the juggernaut hurtled with ever increasing momentum toward the knot of anguished men.

On either side the sleeping houses left neither gaps nor alcoves nor open doors through which the men might escape. The width of the cart was nearly three quarters of the width of the road itself and, although it must leave some men unharmed, the trick would be to estimate precisely against which wall one should hug one's self and hope. At one point the cart snagged against brickwork and the iron bands of its hubs shot visible sparks into the air and threatened to divert the cart to a stop against the wall. But the vehicle broke free, ran across the road, ricocheted off the other side and centered again on its murderous course.

Ren took the only action open to him. Trying to judge the most probable path the vehicle would take, he pressed himself against a wall and prayed. His prayer was not answered. By an apparently willful deviation of its direction the thundering cart moved again across the road and soon was upon him.

Even before the flying wheels made contact Ren knew his injury was going to be savage. The weight and speed of the unattended juggernaut left no doubt of the outcome. When it hit him he was going to be crushed. The heavy axle caught his thigh, and he went partly over the shaft and partly between it and the wall. The shock and pain of so grave an injury was mercifully foreshortened by unconsciousness—but he remembered thinking, as the fringes of darkness closed about him, that with those sort of injuries he would prefer not to live.

Some unknown time later he partially awoke—enough to be conscious of bright flares around him and of an unnatural numbness. He could see Eynes, the surgeon from the spaceport, bending over him, instruments in hand. Somewhere behind the surgeon and barely in focus the red-on-gold emblems of the sick-wagon of the

Society of Pointed Tails danced in the flickering flames. He could hear Di Irons' voice, but could not see him. Ren tried to concentrate on what was being said.

"I'll not let them take him . . . there's not one society hospital in Anharitte has a chance of repairing *that!*"

Eynes cut in plaintively. "We'd need the operating theater facilities of a Stellar Cruiser to save him—and the nearest must be better than three weeks out."

There was another gap in time, then a slight return to consciousness as the whisper of a cushion-craft cut through the enveloping clouds of internal darkness. He caught a glimpse of Eynes' face by torchlight, a picture of worried indecision followed by a shrug and a gesture that meant capitulation. Firm hands gently rocked Ren—next he dimly recognized a pneumatic stretcher that lifted him without movement or dislocation. He experienced a disoriented passage through the air past the bright flames, a moment of unreal eternity he knew he would remember to his death. Then came darkness and a voice like Di Irons' was raging loudly and furiously about his encirclement by fools and villains.

Then nothing—a long, long nothing. He struggled from time to time to break through into consciousness and almost succeeded, only to be defeated by something circulating in his bloodstream. The only thing Ren felt with certainty was that he had not died.

XXIII

Gradually he awoke fully. He was in a bed under sheets of clinical whiteness. Though he feared to explore his condition, the form beneath the fabrics assured him he had not lost his legs. The room was a curved white cocoon, more aseptic and more expensively appointed than any hospital room of his experience. The bulk of smooth equipment at his bedside told of the continuous monitoring of his condition by medical computers.

A door opened and a tall *Ahhn* nurse began deftly to remove the electrodes taped to his wrists and chest and forehead.

"Welcome back to the land of the living, Agent Ren. How are you feeling?"

In an agony of apprehension Ren began to explore himself. A wave of immense relief brought an incredulous smile to his lips.

"I—I'm still complete?" It was a statement as much as a question.

She looked at him sagely. "You've lost a bit of weight, but you'll soon get that back with exercise. You can start getting out of bed today."

"You mean I'm healed?" Ren's voice ran high.

By way of answer she whipped the sheeting from the bed and left him naked to judge for himself. Deep and unfamiliar scars showed just how extensive had been the surgery, yet the flesh was already whole and firm and without unfamiliar sensation except for a slight tingle at the scar-tissue sites.

"You were lucky," she said. "No great internal complications. Your hip bone's partly plastics now, but I doubt if you'd ever have known it if you'd not been told."

"But—how long have I been here?"

"A little over a month." She was amused at his consternation. "You've been kept in medicon-suspension. The healing rate is increased by not having the body constantly in conflict with the psyche. And with a rest from life of that duration, you'll be amazed at how simple your problems have become."

Ren had heard of the technique of this medicon-suspension. Computer-aided instrumentation would have taken over control of his sub-conscious body processes, and his brain would have been allowed to rest. With the computer-enhanced control of his body, a surgeon could promote healing and regrowth at rates otherwise not possible. His body, too, would not have suffered atrophy due to prolonged disuse. The method came from the forefront of medical research on the prime worlds—even there it was available only to the very few who could afford it.

Ren felt good. For the first time in his life he felt completely rested and able to encounter whatever might come with a rational unclouded approach. As the nurse had said, it was amazing how simple his problems had become. He felt as if he were born anew.

"Where am I?" he asked. He knew the answer but wanted confirmation.

"In Magda, of course." The nurse had a way of speaking which reminded him of Zinder.

He watched her carefully. She was an example of pure *Ahhn* stock, yet fully reconciled to the levels of an outworld technology. The result was impressive. Added to her native attributes were a confidence and a competence which fore-shadowed a proud and sane mastery of the future. Ren caught her arm lightly as she reached to disconnect equipment and turned her wrist towards him to see the Magda slave-mark indeli-bly written in her fine skin. But a greater truth was also written there. Dion-daizan's wizardry was a far more potent force than magic.

Now he thought about it, his repair and skilled recovery could only have been due to the re-sources of the man he had set out that night to attack. On all Roget only Dion-daizan could con-ceivably have installed such a facility. The notion made Ren feel slightly sick with himself. Love thine enemy was an old creed to which Ren had not strongly subscribed. Nurse thine enemy back to health with dexterous and expensive skill a modern extension of the idea and one that made Ren, the recipient, feel very humble indeed.

Dion could have left the gates of Magda closed and left his enemy to die on the cold cobblestones of Thirdhill. No one would have thought worse of the *Imaiz* for it. Yet some humanitarian instinct must have prompted Dion to take Ren in and give him a degree of medical attention unobtainable elsewhere in this sector of the galaxy. By this action Dion had revealed his true stature.

Thanks to the effectiveness of his subconscious rehabilitation, Ren felt very little discomfort when he first attempted to get out of the bed. He found his balance lacking, but was able to stand and walk without much difficulty. Considering the extent of the injuries which had brought him down, he knew he had been incredibly lucky.

The *Ahhn* nurse was patient but firm. After a couple of hours of tests and exercises she declared herself satisfied with his recovery.

"You may dress in your own clothes now, Agent Ren. Later Dion-daizan wants to see you."

"I wish to see him, too," said Ren. "I owe him a great deal. But for being admitted here, I should probably have died."

She did not contest the statement, but busied herself in an anteroom dismantling and cleaning the equipment.

"I take it my attack on Magda was a failure?"

"Failure!" Her amusement carried even though he could not see her. "You n̲‥‥‥‥‥ We had a ‥‥‥‥‥ ‥‥ never stood a chance. ‥‥‥ a ring of anti-personnel mines out there that could have destroyed every man you had. And we've everything here from laser rifles to high-velocity flame throwers. But you had organized a peasants' attack, so Dion followed suit. A few things rolled down a hill were all that was necessary to contain you. Take my advice, Agent Ren, and stick to trade. It'll be a long time before there's a force on Roget able to better Dion in a fight of any kind."

Ren dressed, walked to the window and found himself looking out from a position high on Magda's edge. The view ran straight down the valley that divided Firsthill from Secondhill. Small ships were passing through the shipping lanes to and from the great Aprillo river. From this point of vantage Ren's trader's eye could appreciate the vast potential of Anharitte as a landport and as a galactic trading center. In his imagination he re-built the already insufficient dock basin and planned a city more modern but just as pictur-esque and even more colorful on Firsthill.

Almost without knowing it he had begun to identify himself with Anharitte and its inhabi-tants. Local idiosyncrasies were becoming a se-cret source of pride to him. It was the one place in the universe he wanted to think of as home. He wondered if Dion-daizan had looked from a simi-lar window and reached a similar respect for this city built on the three hills.

Ren's resolution was simple now. He was too much in sympathy with Dion's objectives to op-pose the wizard further. He was determined to resign from the Company and remain in Anharit-te. This need not affect his future too much. There were freelance trading prospects on Roget whose potential had scarcely been touched. And if these failed he might even seek employment with Dion himself.

His only fear was that the *Imaiz* might not feel disposed to give him the opportunity to remain. Obviously, from the medical care which had been lavished on him, Dion was not going to exercise his rights over the vanquished and have him exe-cuted. But Ren realized he had been a considera-ble nuisance to the *Imaiz* and he doubted that Dion would suffer him to remain on the planet.

"Agent Ren, the *Imaiz* will see you now."

The nurse had returned and was waiting to escort him. Somehow the slave mark on her wrist no longer seemed incongruous. He saw it now more as a symbol of application and dedication. Dedication to what? The future, perhaps. But training her to such a pitch was no ordinary achievement. It was a measure of Dion's genius. Nobody had ever acquired skills like hers under the coercion of a whip.

He followed her, hoping to get a glimpse of more of Magda's secrets. He was not disappointed. In the corridor he passed the doors of two more hospital rooms and what appeared to be a bio-medical laboratory, all staffed with *Ahhn* nurses and technicians. The end of the corridor brought him back into what was recognizably part of the old castle. The sudden transition from the aseptically clinical to the dark medieval was only a foretaste of the metamorphoses to come.

Dion's hospital had been established high in one of the great flanking towers of Magda. Ren descended some stairs and each level he came to presented to him a tantalizing glimpse of some different technological microcosm. He could hear machine rooms and catch occasional snatches of electronic noise or the smell of chemicals, perhaps from a laboratory. The complexity of pipes and power cables accommodated in the stairwell emphasized just how certainly he had underestimated Dion's potential. Ren was seeing a technical and industrial complex built in minia-ture, but having a manufacturing scope probably unequaled outside of one of the prime worlds.

As he passed along the lower corridors a suspicion grew in Ren's mind. His guide was surely giving him a brief tour of selected parts of the establishment. He surmised that its purpose was to provide him with a more realistic idea of what he would be facing should he again take up arms against the House of Magda—it was also a possible prelude to his pending interview with Dion himself.

Ren took the lesson to heart and found a logical extension. These handpicked and educated slaves of Magda were the new heirs to Anharitte.

They would be the spearhead of a cultural revolution so formidable that the slave system, the societies—and even Di Irons and the City Fathers—were already anachronisms. The marvelous thing about the whole affair was the care that had been taken not to let the old institutions know that they were already dead.

The real question at issue was: how bloody would Dion-daizan allow his revolution to become? Knowledge was power, and Dion seemed to be a specialist in imparting knowledge. Was he also a specialist in controlling this new force he had created? At the moment he was working with a close-knit team and his control of the situation was absolute. But when a wider dissemination of the knowledge came about, as inevitably it must, was Dion big enough still to hold the reins of power?

If he were not, then what would be the cost in terms of loss of life and damage to the essential character of Anharitte?

Magda was built with an outer ward and an inner one containing the great keep. The keep was lower but considerably more massive than the

towers of any of the other castles on the three hills.
As he crossed the inner ward Ren was interested
to note many signs of burning and explosion—
these must have been the result of his own recent
activities. In a way he was gratified to find that his
excursion into improvised weaponry had had
such a powerful result. He had obviously stood
no chance against Dion-daizan, but had he attacked Di Guaard, for instance, he would probably
have won. The notion amused him and he immediately began to feel better about the coming
interview.

On the ground floor of the keep he passed
through a communications center. In it was a
powerful FTL communicator, many times the size
of the limited spaceport equipment. The FTL set
was probably capable of making direct contact
with Terra itself. Suddenly it was no mystery to
Ren as to what had happened to the Rance ships.
Direct intervention by the forces of the Galactic
Federation had stopped them in midflight. Doubt-
less here was the instrument that had broadcast
the alarm.

This consideration placed the galactic standing
of the Imaiz in a new light. Only prime world
governments could afford to build FTL communications equipment and these units were
leased only to those—like space transportation
companies—who had good claim to on-line
communication links across the distances of
space. Dion's acquisition of such an instrument as
this suggested the involvement of outworld
planetary governments in the affairs of Magda.
Rather than being an adventurer, there was a
strong implication that Dion-daizan was an agent

for the Galactic Federation itself.

Ren's previous misjudgment of the situation had been so absolute that he was now incapable of being surprised further. Catuul's attempts to disrupt the *Imaiz*'s estates were made pathetic by radio-telephone links extending widely over provincial Magda. On-line data links coupled to a powerful computer registered and monitored every aspect of the estates' growing and marketing activities. Even the farm-stock prices in the capital city of Gaillen were automatically updated every second.

Dion's knowledge of the overall picture of Roget's outspace commerce was also something that would have made Ren scream in his sleep had he known of it previously. All transactions made through the spaceport communications terminal received an immediate printout in Magda. There still existed an on-line access to all the information contained in the spaceport data banks. A further display of commercial and technological prowess was a broad screen for viewing ship movements on Firstwater—the image of every vessel moved across the screen, accompanied by computer-generated comment on the origin, destination, value and nature of its cargo.

Dion-daizan's chambers were high up in the keep. Ren knocked and was bidden to enter. The chamber into which he came was large and nearly circular, occupying almost the whole area of the level of the keep. The walls from ceiling to floor were lined with books and broken only by narrow windows. Furnishings were sparse and consisted mainly of low wooden stools and the broad desk at which sat the wizard of Anharitte.

"Come in, Agent Ren—be seated. They tell me your recovery is going well."

"Miraculous is the word," said Ren. "I can't thank you enough. But for you and whoever did the surgery I would certainly have died."

"The surgeon, yes—" Dion's eyes twinkled with humor. "He's aged twenty-two and is a native of Anharitte. I bought him as a lad for four barrs. His price was cheap because he wasn't strong enough to carry wood. Still I think it was I who gained the bargain."

"You don't need to spell it out," said Ren. "I was convinced of the effectiveness of your policy the first day I saw Zinder in the market."

"Yet you continued to oppose me?"

"I did. The liberalization of Anharitte appeared inconsistent with the principles of Free Trade. As an agent of the Company I was committed to uphold the Free Trade principle."

Dion-daizan sat back in his chair and interleaved his fingers. Clad in a simple white gown, he might have been the high-priest of a half-hundred religions. But the quiet certainty in his eyes belonged to no fanatic.

"You're a man both of perception and principle," said Dion. "I like that." He leaned over to a communicator on the desk. "Ask Director Vestevaal to join us."

"The director is here?"

"Certainly he's here. He and I have been working while you've been sleeping these several weeks. We've been hammering out a formula to solve our mutual problems."

Magno Vestevaal was in fine form. He greeted Ren jubilantly, inquired about his injuries, then turned back to Dion-daizan.

"Well, Dion, what do you think of him?"

"Much as before," said Dion. "After all, our dossier on him was pretty complete from the moment he was assigned to Roget. The only thing we missed was his profound talent for destruction. Since his coming Anharitte has never been quite the same."

"What's going on?" demanded Ren, looking from the director to the Imaiz and back again.

The director eased himself onto a corner of the Imaiz's desk and turned to Ren confidentially.

"It was the ancient problem, Tito. The irresistible force versus the immovable object: Dion's irresistible climate of social change versus our intractable need for a free port in this sector of the galaxy."

"I'm familiar with the problem," said Ren guardedly. "But it doesn't have a solution."

"It does, Tito—and I've found it. A stroke of commercial genius even if I say it myself. I'd like you to meet a new director of the Company—Dion-daizan."

"A director?"

"Dion's now a major shareholder in the Company and he has been appointed director of sector operations. Don't you see the beauty of it? What he does with his social revolution is no longer our concern. Dion himself is now committed to the principle of maintaining free trade in Anharitte."

Ren felt suddenly bitter. "I can see where the Company stands to gain, but I never thought Dion would sell out the Ahhn for money—" He turned to the Imaiz accusingly.

"Peace, Tito!" Dion-daizan held up a cautioning hand. "Your emotions do you credit, but there's been no sell-out. Freedom and Free Trade are merely different aspects of the same idea of liberty. To assume that they're opposed is a political artifice. It's a fallacy adopted by inept governments to secure an income to which they have no moral title. I always intended the free trade principle to apply to Anharitte. As I recall, it was you who invented the schism."

"I?"

"And think—if I had been genuinely opposed to free trade, do you suppose I would not have removed you as expeditiously as I dispatched the Butcher of Turais?"

"So you think you can integrate the two?" asked Ren. Here were new possibilities for his mind to explore. "On many levels I can see how it would work—but there could be a few fundamental obstacles. For a start I don't see where the societies would fit into the pattern."

"The societies will have to adapt—but then, they're very good at adaptation. They already provide a nucleus of social services, which happily can be expanded. And insurance is an untapped field on Roget. I could almost envy the societies their future." Dion's air of authority was pervasive. He spoke as if the future were under his control.

"Who are you?" asked Ren suddenly.

Dion-daizan grinned broadly. "The wizard of Anharitte, of course."

"He's pulling your leg," said Vestevaal. "He's a Terran sociological engineer provided by the Galactic Federation at the request of the planetary government of Roget. His job is to nurse an essentially feudal society through five hundred years of technological backlog—without its blowing apart or losing its identity."

Ren considered this in silence for a long time, then: "When did you find this out, Director?"

"Unfortunately not till I'd returned from Terra with the *Imaiz*'s contract already signed in my pocket. Dion actually let me conclude the deal before he admitted that what I was buying would have been given freely anyway. In short, he's an even bigger rogue than I. It's a good thing he's now on our side. We didn't do so well with him in opposition."

"And where does this place me?" asked Ren finally. "With Dion in this theater, the Company scarcely needs an agent here."

"My thoughts entirely," said Vestevaal. "In fact I welcomed the chance to take you to Free Trade Central. I wanted to initiate you into the intrigues necessary to maintain a seat on the council. However, Dion has another proposition. He wants you to remain in Anharitte as his personal assistant."

"On Company affairs?"

"Only partially. He also wants you to assist with his program of technical and social reforms. It seems the reputation you have built as Agent Ren, coupled with your deep understanding of the *Ahhn*, gives you the unique ability to serve as a bridge between the two cultures. Both sides know and trust you—and that's a valuable asset indeed. Take a day or two to think it over."

"I don't need a day or two," said Ren. "I had already decided to stay in Anharitte. If Dion will have me, I'm his man. I'm sorry about your plans for me, Director—but I think you understand how I feel."

"No apology necessary, Tito. A few years younger and faced with the same choice, I might even have made the same decision. Anharitte is a place that grows on you. But as it is, I've chosen to take something of Anharitte with me instead."

"Something?"

"I should say 'someone.' It's a sign of the changing times. Dion's manumission bill is going through and he's releasing Zinder from her bond. She and I are to be married on Terra. Then she'll work with me at Free Trade Central. What do you think of that?"

"With a combination of the two of you manipulating the Free Trade Council," said Ren, "I don't think even the merchant worlds will stand a chance."

A NOTE TO READERS

There are a lot more
where this one came from!

Don't Miss these Ace Romance Bestsellers!

_____ #75157 **SAVAGE SURRENDER** $1.95
*The million-copy bestseller by Natasha Peters,
author of Dangerous Obsession.*

_____ #29802 **GOLD MOUNTAIN** $1.95

_____ #88965 **WILD VALLEY** $1.95
*Two vivid and exciting novels by
Phoenix Island author, Charlotte Paul.*

_____ #80040 **TENDER TORMENT** $1.95
*A sweeping romantic saga in the
Dangerous Obsession tradition.*

Available wherever paperbacks are sold or use this coupon.

ace books,
Book Mailing Service, P.O. Box 690, Rockville Centre, N.Y. 11571

Please send me titles checked above.

I enclose $ . . . . Add 50¢ handling fee per copy.

Name . . . .
. . . .
Address . . . .

City . . . . State . . . . Zip . . . .

74B